I0831721

Ranger's Mission

The Rescue Rangers Book 3

Caitlyn Lynch

Shenanigans Press

Contents

Chapter One

The flat crack of a high-powered rifle echoed across the low, rolling hills. No birds startled from the pine trees. They were used to the noise by now.

Glass shattered; one of a row of beer bottles balanced on a wooden rail braced between two oil drums.

Lying on his belly on a low hilltop three hundred yards away, Drew Murphy hissed out a frustrated breath. Moving back from the Barrett sniper rifle leaning on its tripod, he rolled onto his back on the dirt and glared up at the sky, blinking hard. The vision from his right eye remained stubbornly blurry.

His phone vibrated in his pocket, startling him. It had been weeks since he got a call or a message, only carried the phone because he was in the habit of it. Fishing it out, he held it up and squinted at the screen.

Good shot.

Startled, he rolled over, peered back at the bottle-lined rail. A figure emerged from behind the small cabin just to the right, strolled over to the rail and inspected the glass strewn behind it, before turning in his direction and waving.

“Who the hell is that?” Drew’s first instinct was to reach for his rifle and the sniper scope, but he checked himself, groped for his high-powered field glasses instead. A couple seconds later, the figure inspecting the bottles came into sharp focus. “I know you,” Drew whispered, but the man’s name eluded him. One of his fellow Rangers… former fellow Rangers, he corrected himself, with the wrench in his gut which came every time he had the thought.

What do you want? he texted back to the unknown number.

Face to face chat. I brought some replacement beer bottles. Full ones.

Drew was tempted to tell the other man to fuck off, but he was in fact out of beer, and had been wondering whether he could be bothered to make the twenty-mile round trip to town to get some. Some company from a former comrade in arms wasn't a huge price to pay for avoiding the trip for another day or two, at least as long as the guy didn't want to hang around long.

I'll be down shortly, he texted back, and set about breaking down and carefully packing away his rifle.

On the short walk back down to the cabin which had been his home for the last six months, the name of the other Ranger came back to him.

Hunter. Lieutenant Hunter. He left the regiment before I did; went down to Guàlize with Captain MacAulay.

What the hell is he doing up here in Idaho?

Jason Hunter watched the tall, rangy man walking down the hillside with interest. He hadn't known Staff Sergeant Murphy all that well - Drew Murphy was a sniper, and they tended to be solitary types - but from everything he'd heard, Murphy was elite even among Rangers, four times winner of their annual sniper competition. Murphy was the man the top brass sent in when the target absolutely, positively, had to be taken down.

Right up until he got into the middle of a bar brawl, trying to settle down some young recruits scrapping over nothing much, and somebody shoved a broken bottle into his right eye.

Jason's former commander had sent him the medical report which had gotten Murphy his discharge. The eye had been stitched back together by the army's surgeons - Jason shuddered just thinking about it - but the damage was significant. Murphy had less than 20% sight left in that eye, and it was his dominant eye.

Murphy had taken the offered medical discharge and dropped off the grid, apparently winding up here living a pretty rustic life and trying to re-teach himself how to shoot. Jason couldn't quite believe that Murphy had managed to re-train himself using his left eye on the scope, but the shattered glass on the ground behind that rail was pretty compelling evidence.

"Nice shot," he said aloud as Murphy came tramping up the last few steps to the cabin.

"I missed," Murphy said succinctly. "I was aiming for the bottle on the far left end. Hit the third one along. Missed by a damn foot." His right eye showed evidence of the trauma, now Jason was close enough. Pinkish scars below it on his cheek, and the iris looked cloudy grey, as opposed to the clear blue of his left eye. He'd grown a shaggy beard in the last few months, and his skin looked tan and weathered, as though he was spending a lot of time outside.

"You'd best come in, Lieutenant," Murphy said at length, gesturing to the cabin door.

Jason followed him up the rickety couple of steps and inside, glancing around and taking the room in with a comprehensive glance. Inside, it wasn't as run-down as it looked from the outside; the furniture was sparse but in decent condition, a large woven rug covering much of the timber floor.

Murphy laid his rifle case down carefully on the small table in front of the single window, gestured Jason to one of the two chairs. “You said something about beer?” he asked, the ghost of a smile crossing his face.

Jason unslung the pack from his back, setting it on the floor at his feet and fishing out two six-packs.

Murphy pursed his lips in a silent whistle. “European. Hard to find, in these parts, and not cheap. You must want something more than a chat, Lieutenant.”

“You can stop calling me that. I’m not in the Rangers any more.”

“I recall that.” Murphy reached out to take one of the beers, cracked the top and took a long sip. “But I’m not interested in a job in Guàlize. Had quite enough tramping round jungles, thanks.”

“I’m not offering one.” Jason smiled. “Not working there any more myself, as it happens. I'm up here now." He pulled a leather badge case from his pocket, slid it across the table.

"Sheriff of Woodvale?" Murphy's brows raised as he looked at the badge. "That's not far from here. Bet that's an interesting story."

"I'm guessing you don't keep up with the news much," Jason said dryly. "Long story short, I came home to visit my dying great-aunt, discovered her son was a serial killing psychopath and the sheriff was in a human hunting ring with him."

Murphy stared at him, open-mouthed.

"It is in fact a very interesting story, but it's not why I'm here. You can look it all up for yourself. I'm here because I've got a problem and I think you can help me out."

Even though Hunter had claimed to be cutting a long story short, it took him a good half hour to fill in enough details so that Drew started to get the picture. It seemed the entire county sheriff's department had ended up getting suspended, several of them were in jail and the rest were being thoroughly investigated by the FBI as to whether they had any knowledge or complicity in the Manhunters' crimes.

"So you're running the sheriff's department on a wing and a prayer?" Drew asked, about halfway down the third beer.

"And a lot of loaner officers from out of state and other agencies, and a few retired Rangers who heard about my problem and pretty much volunteered themselves. Yeah."

"And you're looking at me as one of those retired Rangers and deciding if I'm not going to volunteer myself, you're gonna recruit me?"

Hunter grinned, took a sip of his own beer - he'd only cracked the one, and was nursing it. "Basically. Yeah. Seems to me you already live here. And the way I see it, you've been sulking about your eye for long enough."

"Sulking!" Drew saw red, slammed his bottle back down on the table.

"Yes." Hunter's stare was unflinching. "We've both known plenty of men who never made it back home at all, or came home with a lot more pieces missing than you did. I've got two in the department missing a leg. So you can't hit a dime at half a mile any more. You're still a better shooter than most guys trying to bag deer. Stop sitting around feeling sorry for yourself and trying to get back something that ain't going to do you any good even if you do."

"You're a shitty therapist, Hunter," Drew said when he got his breath back.

Hunter's grin was wry. "Sorry, man."

"It's all right. I can respect a straight shooter. You're telling it like you see it."

"So." Hunter took another sip of his beer, his eyes watchful. "You interested?"

It had been a long time since Drew has actually felt anything other than frustration and apathy. Deputy sheriff in a small county in northern Idaho was not a life path he'd foreseen for himself, but he could feel interest stirring at the thought.

"Maybe. When would you want me to start?"

Chapter Two

Hunter grinned, sensing victory. Murphy leaned back in his chair, trying to affect casualness, but his voice gave away his interest.

"That's the thing. I'm not going to lie and say I couldn't use you with a badge, on the beat. But."

Murphy arched a brow, abandoning his effort at looking casual. "But?"

"I've been working pretty closely with the FBI, for obvious reasons. But there's a whole alphabet soup of agencies working up here on other things. A few militias about who are on the government's radar. Worrying amounts of opiates on the ground in the area. And one particular biker gang who we know for sure are up to no good, but we can't pin anything on them. The Pure Brethren."

Murphy frowned. "Weren't they an ancient Islamic sect?"

"The Brethren of Purity, but yes. These guys are... not that."

"I'm guessing they lean more towards Aryan Brotherhood ideology?"

"Correct."

"Ack." Murphy made a face like he'd tasted something bad, opened his hand in a gesture for Jason to tell him more.

"Turns out, you have a connection to the Brethren."

"Excuse me? I've never fucking heard of these clowns!"

Jason held out his hands in a 'peace' gesture. "I know. But you inherited this cabin from your cousin Jacob Murphy, right?"

Murphy stiffened. "No. I barely knew Jacob. He left the cabin to our mutual grandmother, who's in a nursing home in Coeur d'Alene. She promptly deeded it to me."

"Came at a handy time, a few weeks before your injury," Jason noted. "Gave you a bolthole."

"Get to the point."

"Your cousin was killed in a shootout in Calgary in a negotiation apparently gone wrong. A drug deal negotiation," Jason clarified. "He was a member of the Brethren. Not just any member; their sergeant-at-arms."

Murphy swore under his breath. "I knew Jacob was a dick. He was always the black sheep of the family. Didn't know he was into shady shit."

"Sorry to be the bearer of bad news." Hunter let him sit with it for a moment.

"This explains the Harley under the tarp in the barn," Murphy muttered.

"Also explains the barn. Or did you not notice it's pretty new and fancy? And your cousin had neither livestock nor machinery to put in it? The Brethren were using it as a storage facility, or a staging post, one or the other."

"Are you wanting me to join them and somehow take up where my cousin left off? I don't see how it's going to work. I told you, Jacob and I barely knew each other. For obvious reasons, now. He thought I was a goody two-shoes and I'd have kicked his ass if I'd known about this Pure Brethren bullshit, never mind the drugs or whatever."

"Or whatever does also come into it," Hunter agreed, smiling wryly when Murphy groaned. "For obvious reasons, the DEA are interested. But it appears that while the Brethren have been running the drugs down from Canada, they are running guns back the other way, so the ATF are involved as well."

"Fuck me," Murphy said eloquently.

"And because the Brethren don't seem to be able to keep their fingers out of any dirty pies they come across, there might be a bit of human trafficking going on too, hence the FBI's interest. And the reason why I'm here. I've been working pretty closely with the FBI. The Area Special Agent in Charge, Agent Carruthers, asked me to approach you because of our shared history with the Rangers, and she authorized me to be completely honest. There is a lot of shit that's gone down here. The last agent the FBI tried to place undercover in the Brethren turned up in my uncle's bone pit. Or some of him did, anyway."

Drew had no idea what to say to that revelation. Clearly Hunter was warning him that things had huge potential to go very far south very fast, if he took the assignment.

"Was your uncle working with the Brethren?" he ventured cautiously.

"Possibly. The former sheriff at least was looking the other way a lot of the time. He's alive, but isn't talking. He's still awaiting trial. Frankly, there is no deal ever going to be offered that will see him avoid death row, but Idaho has only executed three prisoners since 1976. McCarthy will die of old age in prison, and he knows it. He won't talk."

"So we're not going to get that information."

"Not from him. The FBI is still working through the rest of the department, figuring out who knows what, but a lot of them were just dumbly following orders. McCarthy told them the Brethren were law-abiding, the gang took care not to make trouble within the county lines." Hunter shrugged.

"A dead FBI agent says otherwise, but okay. What else? If ATF and DEA are also involved, do they have agents on the ground?"

"Two DEA agents have also been implanted over the last three years; one of them was tragically killed in a crash on the highway late one night. The other fell off a cliff in a hiking accident." Jason's cynical tone made it clear he didn't think either death was accidental. "Neither of them were in place undercover for more than a month, never made it past probationary member status, never found out any real information. The ATF actually had better luck. They got a guy all the way to full member. About a week later, that shootout where your cousin died? Jacob told the agent he knew he was ATF. It was a setup meant for the agent, and by sheer luck, the guy managed to take your cousin down and get away alive."

Drew shook his head, incredulous. "Did they know he was ATF, specifically, though? Or did they just accuse him of being a fed?"

"ATF, specifically, which set spidey senses tingling." Hunter nodded at him, acknowledging that it was a pertinent question. "Particularly since it was only a few days since the ATF had shared information with the other agencies that they had a guy inside."

Drew blew his cheeks out. "There's a mole." It was the only logical conclusion

"At either DEA or FBI. SAC Carruthers says they've pinned it down that far but can't go further right now. ATF have cut intelligence links on the op and are going it alone."

"Can't blame them." Drew smiled wryly, thinking about it. "I don't know," he said finally. "If Jacob ever mentioned me to the Brethren, they're going to know I won't line up with them ideologically."

"That's the interesting thing, though." Hunter smiled, victoriously, like he knew he was about to play a winning hand. "Your cousin did talk about you to the Brethren. Bigged you up. Ranger hero with a Bronze Star and a Purple Heart, all that shit. Never let on that you and he weren't like that." He crossed his fingers and kissed the tips.

"You got this from the ATF guy," Drew guessed.

"Yep. For obvious reasons, he's not hanging around here - any of the Brethren would kill him on sight - but I flew down to Houston, where he's been reassigned, and met him. SAC Carruthers vouched for me to the ATF, and they have given me, and only me, another piece of information. They have another agent in place. Not a gang member, but close enough to observe a lot of their interactions. If you choose to go in, this agent will make contact with you and act as your conduit for any information you have to pass on, while acting as your backup if you need to take action fast, or cut and run."

That actually sounded good. Everyone thought snipers were solo operators, but the truth was that a sniper very rarely operated out in the field without a spotter, watching their back. An ATF agent already in place, knowing the lay of the land, sounded as good a backup as he could ask for, short of another Ranger.

Drew opened his mouth to ask a question, then had second thoughts and closed it again.

"What?" Hunter asked.

"I was gonna ask if I could meet the ATF agent who had to bug out, but now I think on it, maybe it's better I don't. I don't want to let slip something I shouldn't know. Better if I go in blind. Figure out who's who and the lay of the land by myself."

Hunter made a face of distaste. "Not the way we were trained to operate. Any intel is better than none."

"Maybe not if you have to live and breathe an undercover identity, though. I'm going in as myself, but I shouldn't know anything Jacob wouldn't have told me. Where to find them. Who the boss man is. That sort of thing. I need to ask dumb questions if I'm going to look legit, otherwise they're going to realize I know things I shouldn't."

"I get you." Hunter nodded slowly. "How about I have a chat to the ATF agent? Get him to write you a quick brief. The kind of things your cousin might have told you about the Brethren, if you'd been on good terms."

"That works." Drew nodded in agreement.

"So is that a yes… you'll take the job?"

"Let me check. Who am I actually working for?"

"Who's writing the paychecks, you mean?" Hunter grinned.

"Don't care all that much about the paychecks, to be honest." Drew shrugged. "I got a good payout from the army, since I was technically injured in the line of duty, even though it wasn't on the battlefield. I live pretty simply. Don't have anyone to inherit from me except Gran, who's already trying to offload everything she owns onto me. I just want to know who's in my chain of command."

"Me. You can consider yourself officially deputised. I have to keep you off the books for obvious reasons - if the Brethren have someone in the DEA or FBI, they could very well have someone looking at the names on my payroll or at where money going into your bank account is coming from - but we'll agree a pay rate and it will be put in escrow for you until you get clear. Deal?"

Drew looked at Hunter's offered hand. Thought about the alternatives. Sitting here and moping, trying to get back to what he had been before that bar brawl - and for what? It wasn't like he could go back to the Rangers. Hunter was offering a mission. And not only that, but a chance to make reparations for some harm his scumbag cousin had apparently done.

"We have a deal." He reached out, gripped Hunter's hand. "When do I go in?"

"Whenever you want. I'll get that brief from the ATF agent and then leave it in your hands. I'll tell Carruthers I've sent you in, and her counterpart at the ATF who is running the agent who's still in place, but that's it. We'll keep it tightly held - and hope the mole doesn't get wind of what's going on. If at any point you think your cover might be blown, though, run and don't look back. I want you out of there alive once this is all over."

"I hear you." He didn't want to die either. There'd been moments in his career with the Rangers when he'd come close - that Purple Heart was for a bullet which was still rattling around in his abdominal cavity somewhere - but even on his darkest day, the day the surgeons had told him the sight in his right eye was never going to come back any better, Drew had never sought death. He wanted to survive this.

To do some good.

Chapter Three

"Two cheeseburger platters, one full rack of ribs, and a Caesar salad, extra chicken." Liane Hagerty set the plates down on the table, smiled mechanically around at the group who exclaimed with pleasure over the generous portions on their plates, and headed back for the bar, where several regulars were waiting for her to pour their beers. It was a few minutes after noon on a Wednesday, and the kid who waited tables for her at lunchtime was running late, so she was pulling double duty running orders from the kitchen and pouring drinks.

"Sorry, boss!" Merrick ran in the door at that moment, tugging off his jacket and hanging it up on the rack behind the bar. Liane didn't even spare him a glance.

"Wash your hands and get to it," she ordered crisply. "We're busy today."

"You got it, I'm sorry I'm late, my car wouldn't start. Had to wake my mom and get her to give me a ride."

Liane acknowledged the excuse with a nod. Merrick wasn't all that late, but running a roadhouse with a small crew meant a huge extra burden when one of them wasn't pulling their weight. Merrick was a decent kid. He'd get the car fixed up and wouldn't be late again in a hurry.

Motorcycle engines rumbled outside, and Liane took a deep breath. Several of the regulars stationed near the bar stiffened, before drifting away and taking seats at the tables, keeping their eyes carefully averted from the door and the men strutting in as though they, and not Liane, owned the place.

"Afternoon, gentlemen," Liane said affably. "Your usual table is ready for you."

"Nobody else would dare take it," the man at the gang's head replied, smirking. He wasn't particularly tall, but he was broad-shouldered and powerful, his dark hair and beard thickly spattered with gray. His eyes were flat and dead. The gang members called him Bull. Liane didn't know if that was his real name or not. She called him Bull too, if she had to speak directly to him, which she preferred to avoid. The grimy patch on the breast of his leather cut said 'President'.

She watched as the seven men swaggered over to the long table against the far wall of the restaurant, the one by the big window that looked out over the creek which ran down to the lake half a mile distant, her hands busy gathering beer bottles, uncapping them and setting them on the tray Merrick was already waiting to take over.

Nobody kept the Brethren waiting.

Nobody was stupid enough to object when Merrick stayed at their table to take their food orders, either, or when he put the order at the head of the queue to go into the kitchen. Even the couple of groups of tourists who'd stopped off the interstate to get lunch either before or after crossing the border were smart enough to recognize the alpha dogs had just walked into the den.

The roadhouse was busy today, with more folks walking in and looking for tables, but the tables closest to the Brethren stayed empty, with Merrick steering people to more distant tables as they arrived. It was an unspoken agreement that those tables would only be used if the roadhouse was so full there was no other alternative.

There were a lot of unspoken agreements between Liane and the Brethren. Or mostly unspoken, anyway. Back when Liane and her husband Eric had bought the place - before Eric ran off with a waitress half his age, leaving Liane to run the place alone - they'd had a long chat with Bull. It suited Bull to have the roadhouse as his club's hangout, somewhere they got good food and attentive service. It certainly suited the business to have several hungry men regularly eating and drinking there, and Bull had never for a moment suggested that they should pay anything less than full price.

However, Eric and Liane had both insisted on one thing. The Brethren needed to keep their 'business' off the premises. Their very presence was off-putting enough, and it was the regular clientèle that would keep the roadhouse afloat. Anything criminal going on could spell the kiss of death to their liquor license, too, which would shut the roadhouse down even faster.

Bull hadn't liked the condition. He'd tried to push the boundaries more than once, particularly after Eric had left and Liane had stayed on, in charge. Twice she'd walked up to him while he was having a meeting with a stranger wearing different club insignia and bluntly told him to take it out to the car park. She thought he respected her for it, though, and the last time had been several months ago now.

Liane sighed inwardly as one of the bikers rose from the table and came strolling over to the bar, leaning on it, ostentatiously flexing tattooed biceps.

"Finished your beers already, Gerry?" she asked, keeping her tone neutral.

"Just wanted to say how good you're looking today."

She didn't hide her eye roll, saw the scowl roll across his face like a thundercloud.

"Didn't you hear? You shouldn't flirt with women while they're at work. They can't be rude to you for fear of losing their jobs."

"You're the boss. Ain't nobody gonna fire you."

"Just trying to train you into some civilized habits. Please go sit down, Gerry. I know other folks want drinks and won't nobody come to the bar while you're here." She sweetened her tone, allowed a little of the Southern syrup she'd spent years training out of herself back into it. "Look, Merrick's bringin' out your meals. Did you get the ribs today? Ada was pourin' the Jack into the sauce with a generous hand earlier."

Gerry grunted, his eyes raking her up and down with undisguised lust, but he turned around and went back to his seat, grunting a thanks to Merrick as the youth set down his plate.

Liane breathed a quiet sigh of relief that she'd once again deflected Gerry's crude attempts at flirting. One of these days, she was pretty sure he wasn't going to take no for an answer, and she'd have to either appeal to Bull or put

Gerry in his place. She'd rather not have to take the latter option.

The roadhouse was open every day from eleven in the morning until eleven at night, though the kitchen closed at eight. Liane was exhausted by the time she finally finished the cleanup, with the help of the assistant bartender who worked evenings, and headed upstairs to the apartment above the roadhouse where she lived.

Even after a shower and a meal comprised of some leftovers Ada, the cook, had plated up for her, Liane couldn't go to bed, however.

Because now was when her real job started.

Picking up her phone, she settled onto the sagging couch, positioned her fingers carefully and tapped three icons on her home screen simultaneously. The app that opened up belonged to none of the popular social media sites whose icons she had just tapped, however. It was a messaging app, one which wouldn't show up as installed on the phone no matter how much anyone searched. One with only a single contact and a single message thread running.

How was today's take? Liane typed.

Nothing of particular interest, the reply came immediately. There was a sensitive directional microphone installed in the light fitting directly above the Brethren's table downstairs, one whose take was listened to in real time at the local ATF office. And it wasn't the only microphone on the premises; there were two out in the area in the car park where the Brethren parked their motorcycles, and where they always went to conduct their 'business' outside of the bar.

Got some news for you, another message arrived. A new undercover agent is coming in.

"Oh fuck no," Liane said aloud, before typing it into the app, not caring what her boss might think of her language. I'm getting the intel. We don't need another dead DEA or FBI agent. Leave it with me.

Out of my hands. He's already briefed and will be arriving soon. He's not Fed. He's a sheriff's deputy.

"A civilian!" Liane almost shrieked it, her thumbs flying over the screen as she typed.

No. He'll get himself killed. And me. Does he know about me?

He knows there's an agent in place but not who. He's former Army; not a civilian. Make contact when you judge the time is right. You'll be his intel conduit. Your code phrase is 'I think green would be more your color'. He'll respond 'I'm fond of blue, myself'.

It was already in motion, Liane realized dismally, and she had absolutely no chance of stopping it. All she could do was double-check her bugout plans if things went horribly south. When? she asked.

Next few days. Don't have an exact timeframe.

This is bullshit and I'm not happy about it.

Noted, but you know I've never been happy about you being in there all alone. This guy's got a real shot, L. He's Jacob Murphy's cousin.

Her eyebrows just about hit the ceiling at that news. And he's on the level?

Straight arrow.

She wasn't sure she believed it. Jacob Murphy had been Bull's right-hand man, into every bit of the Brethren's business right up to his neck. The one regret Liane had about his death was that Gerry had been promoted to Jacob's former position as sergeant-at-arms, and seemed to think that gave him enough authority to push his luck with her. Other than that, Jacob Murphy's death was a net win for humanity, in her opinion, and she couldn't see any cousin of his being all that decent a human being.

We'll see if he's accepted. Bull's suspicious as hell these days. I'll make contact if he makes it past the first week.

Understood.

Shutting the app down, Liane sighed and hauled herself off the couch, heading for bed and hopefully a few solid hours of sleep before she had to get up. There was a beer delivery due at nine in the morning.

Somehow, she'd never quite imagined that joining the ATF would lead to her running a roadhouse and making a profitable business out of it, but she'd been here a year now, watching the Brethren from as close as anyone could get without actually being a member. Both her 'husband' and the 'waitress' he supposedly ran off with had been other agents, of course, the whole scenario carefully crafted to leave her in place with minimal suspicion attached to her, and it had worked. She acted prickly, fierce, hard-nosed and even bitchy, and the bikers respected her for it, let their guards down around her.

Even the decision to lay down the rule that the club couldn't do business in the roadhouse, a decision she'd queried at the beginning, had been a tactical masterstroke. No undercover agent would do such a thing, they'd actually agreed that in a conversation the microphone had picked up one day. Such an agent would want them where she could keep an eye on them.

Of course, the Brethren had no idea about the microphones in the car park. They meekly obeyed her rule and the ATF still listened to every word they said in their 'business meetings' anyway.

The problem was that the Brethren knew damn well that several different federal agencies were all up in their business, and Bull was a paranoid bastard. Everything was said in vague euphemisms and code, and the information the ATF had gathered so far wasn't significant enough for them to risk Liane's potential exposure by acting on it. They needed 'the goods' and it seemed like the top brass were getting impatient.

Settling into bed, Liane punched her thin pillow in frustration a couple of times, thinking that she really needed to treat herself to a new one. She kept her quarters pretty basic; the roadhouse wasn't exactly turning over enormous profits and extravagance wouldn't fit with the persona she was projecting, even if her personal tastes had run in that direction, but she could damn well treat herself to a new pillow.

Maybe this new undercover agent - cop, she reminded herself, the guy was a sheriff's deputy, not an agent - would finally help her break this case wide open and take the Brethren down.

Even if he got himself killed and she managed to pin it on the Brethren, that'd do, she drifted off to sleep thinking. She wasn't really expecting too much more than that from any cousin of Jacob Murphy's.

Chapter Four

The sound of rain beginning to patter outside made Liane wrinkle her nose and frown, even as she served drinks with her brain on autopilot. The rain meant the Brethren likely wouldn't be in today, spending an easy couple of hundred dollars on food and beer.

A motorcycle engine rumbled throatily outside, as though to contradict her thought, but just the one; Liane frowned as it cut off and silence fell. One thing she'd learned in the last year since taking over the roadhouse, was that the Brethren never, ever rode alone.

A tall figure shadowed the door briefly before entering, the man pulling off his helmet as he crossed the threshold, tucking it under his arm. He wore black leather motorbike gear;

pants and a heavy jacket, and as he turned to survey the room, she saw there was no insignia on the back of the jacket.

This can't be Jacob Murphy's cousin. Surely. He looks nothing like him!

Hard on the heels of that thought came another; Even if he is Jacob's cousin, I have to act like I've never heard of him and treat him like a random biker who's just walked into the Brethren's territory.

So as the man came to the bar, she gave him a hard stare. "You lost, buddy?"

"Not if this is the Redstone Creek Roadhouse, and the sign out front sure seemed to say it is." He leaned on the bar, gave her an easy smile.

Liane tried not to notice how good-looking he was, with sharply chiseled cheekbones not particularly well disguised by the thick stubble on his jaw. It was reddish-blond, a match to his hair, which looked as though it had been very short until quite recently but was now growing out shaggy. He had clear blue eyes - or one of them was. The other looked curiously cloudy, and there was a pinkish scar on his cheek just beneath it.

"This ain't a good place to be hanging out on a Harley unless you're wearing the right colors," she told him bluntly.

"Appreciate the advice." He hooked a bar stool with his heel, slid onto it easily. Set his helmet on the bar. "Could I get a Coors, please?"

"I just told you," she said sharply. "You're not wearing colors. This ain't your place."

"Good thing I'm here to pick some up then, huh?" He smiled at her again.

She stared at him.

"What?" He tilted his head curiously.

"Are you telling me you're here to make an application to join the Pure Brethren? Because you don't just turn up and pick up colors. You have to be accepted. Go through a probationary period. Prove y'all are worthy!"

Jacob Murphy's cousin or not, he was an utter fucking idiot if he didn't know that, and there was absolutely no way she was going to reveal herself as an ATF agent until he'd got himself into a position where he might have some actual, actionable intelligence to pass on.

If he could.

"About that Coors," he said, and she slammed a bottle down on the bar.

"Y'all picked the wrong day to come in."

"Nah," he said placidly, put a ten-dollar note down to pay for his beer.

"It's raining, dumbass!"

"Hadn't noticed." His grin was a little wicked, now, and she thought he was having entirely too much fun winding her up. She scowled blackly.

"Drink your beer and git gone. I don't want word to get around that I let a biker with no colors hang about in my bar."

"You're not gonna get in any trouble. Is that a Southern accent I hear?"

She was annoyed; that was why her accent was coming out. "We're not in the South," she said crisply.

“No, but I spent long enough in Georgia that accent sounds almost like home to me now.”

“Oh, whereabouts in Georgia?” Liane asked without thinking.

“Fort Benning.”

She hesitated. “Army?”

“Rangers.”

That was the final confirmation she needed; this was Jacob Murphy’s cousin, because she’d lost count of the number of times Jacob had bragged about his cousin the Ranger.

“My mother’s from Macon,” was all she said, though, finally picking up his money and going to the cash drawer to make change. “I grew up in Chicago, but folks say I sound like her sometimes.”

“Sure do. ’Specially when you get mad, it seems.” He grinned, and she slapped his change down on the bar with a scowl.

“Word to the wise, buddy. If you’re joining the Brethren, you don’t want to piss me off. Your crew eat in here regularly. Nobody likes spit in their food,” she threatened.

To her surprise, he laughed. “Damn if I don’t like you when you’re mad, too. I’m Drew. Drew Murphy.” He offered a hand to shake.

She eyed it with scorn. Didn’t take his hand and didn’t offer her name in return.

The rumble of motorbikes outside made them both look towards the window. Drew didn’t seem worried; she guessed he’d made contact somehow with someone from the Brethren and they’d agreed to meet him here, though from everything she knew about them, there was no way Drew was going to be welcomed in with open arms, not even with his relationship to Jacob in his favor.

“Hope you weren’t bullshitting about them expecting you. If you were, you’ll be taking your business outside, or I’ll be calling the sheriff and gettin’ him to impound your bike until you compensate me for any damages,” she warned.

“On good terms with the sheriff, are you?” He raised his brows. “Unusual. For the owner of a biker hangout.”

“We serve the best barbecue in the damn state, so yes. Sheriff and plenty of his deputies eat here regularly, and the Brethren keep a respectful distance and their noses clean while they're on my property." Her tone was threatening. Warning him that he needed to respect her rules.

"Interesting." He nodded at her, and then rose to his feet as the door opened to admit Bull, Gerry hard on his heels, the rest of the Brethren streaming in behind them.

"Don't want no trouble in here, Bull," Liane said as Bull strode up to Drew. "Take it outside." Her tone was a lot more polite and respectful than it had been when she was speaking to Drew, but it was still firm.

"No trouble, Liane. This is a welcome guest," Bull said, before holding his hand out to Drew. "Hey, Drew. I'm Bull. Jacob spoke very well of you."

"It's an honor to meet you, sir. Jacob talked like the sun shone out of your ass."

Bull laughed, a deep, rolling belly laugh, and gestured towards the Brethren's table. "Come and join us. That's our table, over there; Liane keeps it reserved for us special, don't you?"

“Only the best for my best customers,” Liane said, but she kept her tone cool. She didn’t fawn and the Brethren knew not to expect it. “What are you drinking today, Bull?”

“Is the Grand Teton Double Vision Doppelbock in stock?”

“Sure is, got the delivery yesterday.”

“Let’s have a round of those, then.”

Bull drank Budweiser as often as not, but clearly he wanted to appear cultured - or perhaps affluent - in front of Drew Murphy. Interesting. She had to concede Murphy was quite an impressive specimen; about six foot two and solidly muscled, it was the way he moved which set him apart. Like a rattlesnake on the verge of striking, she thought whimsically as she took the beer bottles from the cooler, watching from the corner of her eye the men taking their seats at the window table. Bull took the seat at the head, gesturing Murphy to his right hand, which earned a scowl from Gerry who normally sat there.

Merrick was busy taking orders from a table full of women who were having a book club meeting, of all things, and had apparently decided to combine that with lunch, so Liane put seven bottles on a tray and carried them over to the Brethren's table, serving Bull first.

"Six Grand Tetons, one Coke." She put the soda bottle down in front of Kaleb, Bull's nephew, who despite being just as tattooed and rough-looking as the rest of the gang, hadn't turned twenty-one yet. He'd tried, just once, to show her a fake ID. She'd taken one look at it and said "I ain't risking my liquor license for you, kiddo."

Kaleb rolled his eyes but knew better than to say anything.

Drew shot a curious look along the table. "You teetotal or something?"

"He's underage," Liane said, "and whatever you folks do outside of this place, in my bar we are all law-abiding citizens. Ain't that right, Bull?"

"That's right." Bull grinned, and as she walked away, he said quietly to Drew "She's a hardass, but this place has the best food for miles around. Think of it as a safe space. Like a church sanctuary."

Liane smiled a little to herself. She quite liked the analogy. The smile disappeared as she heard Drew's answer.

"Hardass, but she's sure got a nice ass."

Undercover persona, she had to remind herself. Drew was playing a part, and so was she. Turning around, she wagged her finger at him.

"Window shopping's free, but any man who tries to touch the goods is gonna wind up with a broken finger."

"Noted, ma'am," Drew answered with a grin. Bull was chuckling, as were several of the others; Gerry's expression was black as thunder though, she saw.

It occurred to Liane then that a flirtation with Drew would be the easiest and most logical way for them to easily exchange information. Of course, he didn't know yet that she was his ATF contact - and she didn't plan to let him know unless and until he was accepted by the Brethren - but she could certainly lay some groundwork. Deliberately, she winked at him before turning around and heading back to the bar.

She couldn't listen in real time to the take from the microphone at the Brethren's table, of course, and she didn't want to watch them too obviously, but she kept a weather eye on the group as she went about her work, watching body language for the most part.

Drew looked relaxed, untroubled by the fact that he was eating and drinking with hardened criminals. Bull seemed expansive, smiling more than he usually did, laughing and listening intently to Drew when he spoke. Gerry's scowl grew blacker by the minute.

Kaleb was the interesting one. Bull thought a lot of his nephew, and Kaleb was hanging on Drew's every word, nodding eagerly in agreement when he spoke. Jumping to his feet and beckoning to Merrick when Drew tapped the laminated menu on the table and obviously asked a question about ordering food.

Merrick was right in the middle of delivering plates to the book club's table, and shot Liane a faintly desperate look. She nodded to let him know she'd catch it and went back to the Brethren's table, fishing an order pad from her jeans back pocket.

"What's the special today, Liane?" Bull asked affably.

"Chicken-fried steak with buttermilk biscuits and gravy," she said.

"You got a Southern cook too, Georgia girl?" Drew asked, and she narrowed her eyes at him.

"Told you, my mother was the Georgia girl, not me. But yes. Ada's from Alabama and if you like Southern cooking, you'll probably be crying into her biscuits by the time you've finished lunch."

"Can you even make proper biscuits with the flour up here?" he riposted.

"No, which is why we get White Lily shipped up from Knoxville!" She smirked at him, and he smiled back, nodding.

"All right, you convinced me. Chicken-fried steak sounds good."

"Same for me," Kaleb said quickly, and Bull tipped up a finger, indicating he wanted the special too.

“Another round of beers too,” Bull requested, and she nodded, quickly noting down the other men’s orders.

“Won’t be but a few minutes, I’ll just run these to the kitchen.”

Merrick was free by the time she’d delivered the food order and prepared the drinks, so she let him take the tray over. It didn’t do to give the bikers too much personal attention. It didn’t fit with her abrasive undercover persona, and it might make Bull suspicious if she was hovering over them all the time.

Chapter Five

Yet again, Drew found his eyes being drawn to the bartender's shapely ass, as she leaned over a table on the other side of the room collecting up dirty glasses. Cursing himself mentally, he dragged his gaze away and forced himself to focus on what Bull was saying. He really couldn't afford to get distracted right now.

Still, Liane was the most fascinating woman he'd met in a long time. Tall - he bet she was five ten in her bare feet - and sturdy, she had a narrow, clever face, clear blue eyes and a gamine pixie cut, which might have made her look cutesy except for the fact it was dyed purple with black tips. In skintight blue jeans, heavy Doc Marten boots and a black flannel shirt over a white T-shirt, she was the epitome of a tough girl, all sass and sharp edges.

...And soft curves...

Christ, I'm staring at her again.

Even worse, she'd just caught him at it as she turned around. Raising an eyebrow, she grinned and tipped him another saucy wink.

"Didn't the Rangers teach you no self-preservation, boy?" Bull asked, obviously following Drew's stare. "She'll chew you up and spit you out."

"Might be worth it." He laughed, trying for self-deprecating. "I think I was out in the desert too long on my last tour."

"When did you say you got back, again?"

"About two weeks after Jacob was killed." Which happened to be a fortuitous coincidence, not that Bull could know that. "I was damn sorry to miss his memorial. I hope you sent him off right."

"We did." Bull's expression was hard to read, behind his thick beard, but Drew actually thought it might be one of grief. "Scattered his ashes at his favorite fishing spot, like he wanted."

"He always did love fishing," Drew agreed. It was probably the thing he remembered best about his cousin, Jacob forever running out on the small chores their grandmother set them to go fishing.

They finished their meals, and Bull leaned back in his chair, fixing Drew with a sharp stare. "It's been nice to meet Jacob's cousin, but I feel like you didn't call me up and ask to meet here just to reminisce about him. Let's get to business."

"We can't talk business in here, Bull," Kaleb piped up. "Liane's rules."

"Different kind of business, kid. Hush your face." Gerry nudged the boy and growled.

Drew noted from the corner of his eye Kaleb's flush, Bull's frown at Gerry. The internal dynamic between the gang members was something he needed to be hyper-aware of; he wished the ATF agent who'd formerly been undercover had provided more information on it. Maybe his new contact would be able to fill him in on some details, when he got in touch.

“I inherited Jacob’s cabin,” he answered Bull’s question, “and his bike. Don’t have anywhere to be in particular now I’m out of the service. Figured here’s as good a place to settle as anywhere. I got a decent payout but I’ll be needing to look for work soon, and if I’m riding Jacob’s bike… well, it seemed like only courtesy to inform you that I’m here, and I’ll be on his bike.”

“How’d you get my number?” Bull asked interrogatively. “It’s not something Jacob would have given out to anyone. Not even family.”

“No doubt, but all his old phone bills were in a filing box. I just dialed the number he called most often, and you answered. Wasn’t hard to figure out it’d be your number, the amount he always talked about you.”

Bull nodded, accepting the story. As well he might, because it was the absolute truth. For long moments he considered Drew in silence. Drew waited, keeping his expression smooth and unruffled.

Patience was one of his greatest strengths. He'd lost count of how many hours and days he'd spent lying in deeply uncomfortable positions, waiting for the chance to take his shot.

Nobody could out-wait a sniper.

Certainly not some two-bit biker from rural Idaho.

"What kind of work d'you plan to look for?" Bull asked finally.

"Something where it doesn't matter that I can't see worth a damn out of this eye." Since the injury, Drew had developed something of a nervous tic, stroking the scar tissue under his right eye. It didn't hurt any more, but the skin felt subtly wrong, not just the slight ridge of the scarring under his sensitive fingertip, but the sensation his brain registered from the touch too.

"Can you operate any heavy machinery?" Bull asked.

Wondering where the biker was going with this line of questioning, Drew shook his head.

"Can't say I've ever driven anything heavier than a pickup truck."

"Then I think you're going to struggle to find anything. Most jobs around here are in logging or farming. You might find something down at Sandpoint."

"Huh." Drew folded his arms, frowned. "If I wanted a commute, I could have stayed in Georgia. Not keen on working in a city either. A desk job sure as hell ain't going to suit me."

"I hear that." Bull toasted him with his beer bottle, beady eyes watching him keenly. "I might be able to offer an alternative, if you were interested."

"I'm all ears."

"The Brethren do some business, as a group, locally. We can always use another good man."

"You inviting me to join?" Drew raised his brows, surprised.

"You can't just offer him full membership, Bull," Gerry blustered. "There's a probationary period. We don't waive that for anyone. Hell, we didn't even let Kaleb off it!"

“Drew went through Ranger training. Don’t think anything we can throw at him during probation is gonna faze him too much, do you?” Bull smirked.

“I’m sure as shit not going to put up with any hazing, so if you’ve got plans for that, forget it,” Drew said flatly, meeting Gerry’s scowl with a hard stare.

“Nothing like that,” Bull said, too quickly, so that Drew knew hazing was indeed a usual part of whatever probation the Brethren put prospective members through. “It’s just... earning our trust.”

“I can understand that.” Drew nodded, working hard on looking casual. “Jacob would have vouched for me, of course, but he’s not with us.”

“Bull,” Gerry said urgently, “can we talk outside?”

Bull sighed, but he nodded, pushed back his chair and followed his sergeant-at-arms outside. Drew relaxed back in his chair, crossing his ankles, trying to give off an unworried air. He caught himself looking at Liane again and snatched his gaze away.

“I was Jacob’s prospect,” a voice said quietly beside him, and startled, he looked around to meet Kaleb’s eyes. Bull had made quick introductions, and Drew had taken note that the youngest member of the Brethren was Bull’s nephew.

“Was he good to you?” was all Drew could think to ask.

“He was. Firm but fair.”

Drew privately thought that didn’t sound at all like his cousin. His strongest memories of Jacob were the summers the two of them had spent on their grandparents’ farm; Jacob, two years the older, had been an absolute bully. At least until Drew got big and strong enough to fight back.

“If Bull says you can join,” Kaleb said, “I’ll ask if you can be my prospect.”

Drew took a moment to formulate his response. He had to be at least a decade older than Kaleb, and it seemed faintly ridiculous to effectively apprentice himself to a kid who barely looked old enough to shave.

On the other hand... Kaleb was likely privy to a lot of the Brethren's secrets. Bull might let his guard down more around the kid, let slip information he otherwise might not, because Kaleb was family.

"Looking out for me, like Jacob looked out for you?" Drew asked finally.

"Something like that." Kaleb ducked his chin, a little sheepishly.

"I'd be honored," Drew said, watched the blush spread across Kaleb's face.

The kid sat up a little straighter.

"Gerry's got a problem with me, and I want to know why." Drew kept his voice low, pitched for Kaleb's ears only. "Did he and Jacob have beef?"

"Nah, it's because you were in the military." Kaleb's answer was quick.

Confused, Drew blinked. "What?"

"Gerry was in for two years, but they kicked him out. He don't talk about why." Kaleb spoke quietly too. "He's a sovereign citizen. You know what that is?"

“I do. Are the rest of you sovereign citizens too?” Drew asked.

“No, though Gerry keeps trying to talk us all into it. Bull says it’s crap. Gerry believes every damn conspiracy theory he hears; it gets exhausting after a while.” Kaleb rolled his eyes.

Drew suppressed a laugh, then changed his mind and let out a low chuckle. “So. Let me guess. Gerry thinks the military is the tool of the lizard overlords?”

Kaleb choked on a sip of soda, before bursting out laughing. “Something like that,” he snickered, but quieted as Bull and Gerry returned to the table.

Gerry looked sullen, fists clenched at his sides. He shoved his chair back against the table and stayed standing, leaning on the back of it.

Bull overruled him, Drew thought. Obviously, there was no blackball rule in the Brethren… though Drew suspected that didn’t apply to Bull. If the president had been the one who didn’t want Drew in, he’d have no chance.

But Bull was smiling at him.

"We cool?" Drew kept his eyes on Bull, ignoring Gerry. The fact that the club president and sergeant-at-arms didn't see eye to eye on all matters was possibly something he could use, a crack to leverage to his advantage, but he had to pick a side, and Bull was the obvious choice.

"We're cool. You can join as a prospective member, a prospect. One of the full members will take you on..."

"I want to take him on as my prospect," Kaleb said quickly.

Gerry snorted with laughter. "You?"

Bull turned to give Gerry a hard stare. "You implying my nephew ain't just as capable as any other full member?"

The other men further down the table were scowling too, Drew noticed from the corner of his good eye. Kaleb was obviously popular among the other members of the Brethren; Gerry less so.

"Wasn't saying that, Bull," Gerry said quickly.

"You better not have been."

The words were said quietly, but with an air of such menace Drew had to suppress a shudder. It was a good reminder; that for all his apparent affability, Bull and his gang had left a trail of dead bodies in their wake, and if they for one moment suspected Drew wasn't exactly what he appeared to be, he could well join the ranks of their victims.

"Anyone else care to volunteer?" Bull asked after a long moment of dead silence, looking away from Gerry and along the table. One by one, all the other men shook their heads.

"Kaleb's capable," a thin redhead with a scruffy beard at the end of the table said. The patch on his cut read Secretary, Drew spotted now, and resolved to learn the redhead's name. "He knows what's required."

"All in favor of Kaleb taking Drew on as his prospect?" Bull asked. Every man raised their hands, including Gerry, although he was slow and obviously reluctant about it. "Settled, then. Get him a cut and give him the tour, Kaleb. He needs to learn where everyone lives. Oh, and take care of the tab!"

Chapter Six

Everyone was standing, obviously getting ready to leave, so Drew stood up too, suddenly wondering if Bull's order to take care of the tab had been directed at him. The roadhouse wasn't a pricy type of place, but they'd had three beers and a full meal each, multiplied by seven men; the check was going to be a couple of hundred dollars at least. Kaleb, though, was fishing a thick roll of bills from his front jeans pocket, peeling several off as he headed for the bar.

"All together?" Liane asked as Kaleb stopped in front of her, "or is he paying his own way?" She nodded towards Drew.

"He's one of us now," Kaleb said. "Heading out to go pick him up a cut."

She nodded, apparently disinterested. "Two hundred and eight and change."

Kaleb put a stack of bills on the bar. "Keep the change."

She nodded, a small smile touching her lips as she swept the money off the bar. Kaleb had put two hundred and fifty dollars down, Drew thought, and not only that, he'd spied most of the gang members putting fives and tens under their plates for the servers to collect when they cleared the table. The roadhouse did pretty well off the Brethren; perhaps it was a bit surprising Liane wasn't more accommodating.

He also had to wonder where all that cash was coming from. Too early to start asking those sorts of questions, though, so he just smiled politely at Liane and said;

"You were right about those biscuits, ma'am. Haven't had biscuits that good since leaving Georgia."

That little smile touched her lips again. "I'll tell Ava you enjoyed them," she said, with a little tip of her head, before she turned away, obviously dismissing him.

"Come on," Kaleb nudged Drew's shoulder, and he realized he'd just been standing there, watching Liane walk away.

Kaleb was snickering quietly. "You've really got the hots for her, huh?"

"What can I say, I like confident women," Drew said with a shrug, trying to laugh it off. "She's gorgeous."

"Bit old for my taste," Kaleb said, grinning. "You might have to fight off Gerry, though. He's been trying to hit on Liane ever since her husband ran off with their old waitress. Before, actually, I think."

"If he hasn't made any headway in all that time, I don't think he's actually much competition," Drew pointed out as the two of them left the roadhouse. The rain had stopped, leaving everything slick and shining, the scent of the pine trees behind the roadhouse heavy on the air. "He clearly doesn't like me anyway."

"He doesn't like anyone much. Watch yourself, though." Kaleb said no more, just headed over to where the bikes were parked, just their two left now.

"Where are we headed first?" Drew asked, putting his helmet on.

"Cash's place. Get your cut."

"Cash?"

"The secretary. Redheaded guy, at the end of the table?"

"Oh, yeah." Drew nodded. "Well." He kicked the starter, grinned as the Harley's engine roared to throaty life. "Lead the way!"

Cash turned out to live right in town, in a neatly maintained house with an attached garage. His bike was nowhere in sight, and Drew thought as he and Kaleb parked theirs on the driveway that from the outside, there was nothing here to suggest the house belonged to a motorcycle gang member.

"Hey, Cash," Kaleb rattled his knuckles against the door.

"It's open!" a voice yelled from inside the house, and Kaleb opened the door to let them in.

They went through into a surprisingly nice living room. Drew suspected Cash was married, or at least lived with a woman; the inside of the house was far too nice to be a bachelor pad, with bright cushions on the chairs and a handmade quilt neatly folded on the back of the couch.

"Hey." Cash was sitting on the couch, boots off, feet resting on the coffee table in front of him. "There's a couple of cuts there." He gestured to a side table. "Try them on for size."

The first leather vest was made for someone broader in the shoulders than Drew: it slid about uncomfortably. The second fitted better, and he nodded, brushing his fingers lightly over the Prospect patch on the breast. "This one. Thanks."

"Your phone." Cash made a beckoning gesture with his fingers.

"Say what?"

"Hand. Over. Your. Phone."

Reluctantly, Drew fished it from his pocket and held it out. There was nothing incriminating on it - and they wouldn't be able to unlock it without his fingerprint anyway

- but he wasn't particularly keen on just handing it over.

"While you're a club prospect, you use this one. I know there ain't no landline at Jacob's cabin. You won't be making any calls we don't know about. All our current numbers are already saved for you." Cash took Drew's phone, tossed it into a drawer he opened in the coffee table, and handed back an older-style flip phone.

"Does this even have internet access?" Drew grumbled, opening the phone and looking with disgust at the tiny screen.

"What d'you need that for? You can go to the library if you want to check your email. Kaleb will tell you anything else you need to know. Now git gone before my woman gets home. She don't like to see bikes parked on the driveway."

"You're henpecked, Cash," Kaleb said teasingly, and to Drew's surprise, the redhead cracked a smile.

"One day you'll meed the right woman, kid, and you won't mind being a little bit henpecked."

The club seemed to view Kaleb as something of a mascot, Drew thought, for all he was a full member. The kid seemed pretty decent - a thought he revised as they left Cash's house and Kaleb said they needed to drop by the high school.

"What for?" Drew stared at him, puzzled.

"Gotta pick up my girlfriend."

I hope this isn't going where I think it's going. "She a teacher?"

"Nah, she's in the tenth grade."

"Jesus, you want to go to jail? She's gotta be underage!"

"We don't do nothing." Kaleb rolled his eyes. "She says I'm too old for her too. She acts my girlfriend because it's good cover, and her parents don't care."

"Cover?" Drew was utterly lost. "For what?"

"She's our dealer in the school, man. Moves plenty of product."

Oh. So he's not having sex with a teenage girl. He's just using her to deal drugs to other kids.

It was a cold, hard reminder that no matter if some of the Brethren might seem personable, even likable like Kaleb, they were criminals with a sociopathic lack of regard for anyone they didn't consider worthy of their attention.

The feds surely knew about Kaleb's girlfriend being the high school drug dealer already - it was pretty hard to miss Kaleb roaring up on his bike to pick her up - but Drew still mentally filed it away as a snippet of information he could pass on once the undercover ATF agent made contact. It wasn't like he had any other avenue of passing on information the Brethren wouldn't be aware of, bar taking a ride down to Woodvale and going into the sheriff's office to find Jason Hunter. Something which would very much be a last resort, because who knew who might be watching and reporting back to the Brethren.

Kaleb's 'girlfriend' was a pretty blond cheerleader - literally a cheerleader, in a blue and white uniform. She jumped on the back of Kaleb's bike, waving to her friends, and they roared off again.

They took Kaleb's girlfriend home, where she skipped off inside without even a backward glance. Drew had seen the exchange taking place as they rode, the girl tucking a wad of cash into Kaleb's jeans pocket and taking out a small package in return which she stuffed into her bra.

It was starting to rain more heavily again, so Kaleb suggested they stop by his place for a while.

"You got your own place?" Drew asked curiously.

"Yeah. It's not all that big but it's all mine."

They were parked up at the gas station, fueling their bikes. Kaleb pointed out the mechanic's shop attached, noting that there was an excellent bike mechanic working there if Drew needed anything doing on his bike he didn't feel confident doing himself.

"Though we'll need to check your bike over afterwards," Kaleb added. "In case of any trackers or bugs he might have put on. We haven't caught him at anything yet, but Bull thinks he might be an undercover agent, planted to keep an eye on us. Only moved here a few months ago."

Drew had been just about to say that he didn't think there was any mechanical work his bike might need that he couldn't handle, but he changed his mind on hearing Kaleb say that. If the mechanic was indeed the ATF undercover agent, Drew needed to give him an opportunity to make contact - and then to warn him that the Brethren were suspicious.

"She's alright for the moment," he said, "but she'll want new tires soon. I'll get him to do that, at least."

"They give us a good price on tires." Kaleb nodded. "C'mon, let's go. We'll pass by Bull's place on the way to mine."

Bull's place was as nondescript from the outside as Cash's; bigger and slightly newer, but not quite as immaculately clean. A new black F150 with massive dually tires was parked on the driveway.

"Is Bull married?" Drew asked as they got off their bikes outside Kaleb's house, a small, slightly scruffy brick bungalow.

"No," Kaleb said shortly. "He was. She disappeared, a couple of years ago. He thought she left him. Turned out, she was murdered by the Manhunters. They found her remains in that bone pit."

"No! How awful for Bull. That's a hell of a thing, huh? Serial killers operating right in your backyard. Did you know any of the guys involved?" It was only natural to want to talk about the topic, Drew thought; it would be weird if he didn't show an interest. Drew felt cold, though, knowing that the body of an FBI agent who'd been undercover with the Brethren had also turned up in that bone pit. Had Bull handed his own wife over to Philip Hunter's crew of killers, as well as the agent? Did Kaleb know?

"Yeah," Kaleb admitted gruffly. "The former sheriff, McCarthy. He's how the Manhunters were able to get away with it for so long. Covered their tracks, y'see."

"Pretty sick." Drew shook his head.

"Wouldn't necessarily have thought you'd see it like that." Kaleb gave him a sidelong glance as they entered the house.

"Why?"

"You were a sniper, man. You've probably killed more people than the whole crew of Manhunters did."

"Maybe I did - I didn't keep a tally - but they were enemy combatants," Drew pointed out. "Taliban, for the most part. A few Somali warlords. Scum of the earth, people with blood on their hands. The Manhunters killed old folk, women, kids. Innocents. It's very different."

"If you say so." Kaleb shrugged, leading the way into a small kitchen and opening a pantry door. "Want some chips?" He pulled out a large package. "I'm hungry."

"Already? Lunch wasn't all that long ago." Drew shook his head when Kaleb thrust the packet in his direction. "I'm good, thanks."

"I'm still growing." Kaleb grinned and threw some chips in his mouth. "C'mon. Let's sit down. See what's on TV."

Hanging around watching TV didn't feel like he was doing much of a job as an undercover agent, but Drew rationalized that he was, actually - he needed to get Kaleb comfortable and relaxed with him, and that would be easier the more Kaleb thought they had in common. With an inward sigh, he settled onto Kaleb's couch and put his feet up on the coffee table, imitating the younger man. "You got cable? Jacob's cabin is too far out of town for it. I miss ESPN."

"Sure." Kaleb tossed him the remote. "Knock yourself out. And I got a spare room, if you don't feel like riding back home. Bed's yours any time."

"Appreciate that." He'd take Kaleb up on the offer intermittently, Drew decided. It showed trust, and he needed Kaleb to believe the trust went both ways.

Even though Drew knew that he could never, ever trust any one of the Brethren for even a moment.

Chapter Seven

Liane took a deep breath as motorcycles rumbled on the gravel outside the roadhouse. It had been two weeks since Drew Murphy first walked in to meet with the Brethren. He'd been into the roadhouse with them several times since, apparently completely comfortable in their company, and her ATF bosses had finally lost patience and ordered her to make contact with him, identify herself and retrieve any information he might have gathered so far.

He'd certainly had plenty of opportunity to pick up some useful intelligence, Liane thought as she watched the bikers swagger in. He seemed to have spent every moment in Kaleb's pocket. The Brethren ate in the roadhouse at least four or five days a week and Drew was always with them, listening quietly and running small errands like a good, hardworking prospect should.

Drew was the one who came to the bar now, offering his usual flirtatious smile as he ordered a round of beers.

“Plus soda for Kaleb,” Liane said.

“You taken note of when his birthday is? Not far away.”

“Three months, and until then, he ain’t drinking alcohol in my bar.” She paused, looking at him. Psyching herself up. Now was the moment, but how to do it?

Flirting with him - even pretending to start a relationship - would actually be excellent cover for them. She leaned on the bar, looking into his eyes, and took another deep breath before saying; “I like that bandanna you’re wearing. But I think green would be more your color.”

It clearly took Drew a couple of seconds to register that she’d spoken the code phrase he’d been told to expect from his ATF agent contact. And then his eyes flew wide open and he stared at her, lips parting with obvious shock.

Liane raised a brow at him.

“Uh,” he said, clearly needing a moment to reorient his worldview. “I - I’m partial to blue, myself.”

She leaned closer. “Flirt with me,” she said softly. Nobody was close enough to hear, right that moment, and the smile she had on her face would look coy to any onlooker. “It’s good cover. Gives us an excuse to spend time together.”

“Right.” He still looked a bit shell-shocked: Liane had to wonder who exactly he’d thought his contact might be, because it couldn’t be more obvious that he hadn’t for a moment suspected her. “I guess we need to talk.”

“Buy me a drink?” She raised her voice, then laughed loudly. “I own the bar. You’ll want to come up with a better line than that, hotshot.”

“Can’t blame a guy for trying.” He leaned on the bar and smiled at her, flashing a sudden, unexpected dimple in his cheek. “The drink’s just an excuse. I want to get to know you. You name the time and place."

She pretended to think about it. "Be here at five when my substitute bartender gets in. We'll talk... if I get time."

"You got it." He winked. "Should I bring flowers?"

"I prefer chocolate."

"Noted." Scooping the tray of drinks off the bar, Drew headed off to the Brethren's table without a backward glance. She wondered what he'd say to them - he'd have to say something to explain why he was coming back here without them - and didn't have to wait long to deal with the consequences. Gerry came storming up to the bar, shoving two young construction workers waiting patiently for their drinks aside. One of the guys opened his mouth to argue; his friend, obviously smarter, or at least with a greater sense of self-preservation, dragged him quickly away.

"You would never give me the time of day, but you're giving that cunt Murphy a shot?" Gerry snarled, banging his hands down on the bar.

Liane met his eyes squarely, determined not to back down. "I've told you plenty of times, Gerry. You're not my type."

"What's that supposed to mean?"

"You drink too much, you cuss too much, you undress every woman who walks past you with your eyes, and according to more than one of your ex-girlfriends, you've got a mean streak. Very much like my ex-husband, in fact. I'm not into repeating my worst mistakes." Liane nodded to where Drew was handing beers around the Brethren's table. "He's polite. Yeah, he stares at my ass all the time - but it's pretty much only my ass. He ain't in here looking at every girl who shoves her tits in his face." Which was curious, she suddenly thought, since he'd obviously had no clue she was his ATF contact. Maybe he was actually attracted to her.

Gerry huffed and puffed, and then a nasty smirk crept across his face. "Murphy's a prospect. Has to have permission to start a relationship with anyone."

"One, who said anything about a relationship? We're gonna have a conversation. And two, you're making yourself look jealous and pathetic. Go find a woman who's interested in you and butt out of my life." She met him glare for glare, and a little to her surprise, Gerry looked away first, snorting with disgust. He stormed off towards the bathroom, leaving Liane feeling a little shaky after the confrontation, not that she allowed it to show outwardly. Instead she looked at the Brethren's table, not looking away until Bull happened to glance at her. She scowled at him.

Bull gave an obviously exaggerated sigh, but he stood up and came over to the bar, leaning on it. "Got a problem, Liane?"

"Leave me out of your bullshit," she said without preamble. "I like Murphy, and he seems to be interested, but I don't want to get caught up in Brethren business. Gerry said, because Murphy's a prospect, he has to have permission to date me?" Her tone made it clear what she thought of the rule.

"We don't want him distracted from club business... and we'd need to vet anyone he gets involved with. Make sure they're not a threat to us."

Liane gave him a hard stare.

"Of course we already vetted you, so that wouldn't be a problem," Bull said with an unconcerned shrug.

"Well." She wiped the top of the bar with a damp cloth. "I can't imagine that a decorated Ranger sniper is the easily distracted type."

"Me neither, but if we have to tell him to break it off with you, just know, it's nothing personal, Liane."

"It's personal for Gerry." She went straight to the heart of the problem. "He's not good at taking no from me, and he's gonna try and make it difficult. Y'all need to keep him off my neck... and not let him hassle Drew, either."

Bull gave her a sharp look. "Don't mistake our friendly working relationship now, Liane. You don't get to give orders. I'll handle my people my way."

Ah. It was the first time Bull had pushed back, really. She ducked her head submissively. "Don't mean any disrespect, Bull. Just don't like people all up in my personal business. Or my business business, come to that."

"I know. And we've stayed out of your running this place, because frankly you seem to be doing a good job of it. But you get personally involved with one of us, you can't stay neutral. This ain't Switzerland."

Liane privately thought that was a pretty complex concept for the biker to express, but she nodded. "Just want to see if he's worth spending any time on. Might not come to anything."

"Fair enough." Bull nodded, peering at her thoughtfully. "Two weeks. If you want to pursue anything with Murphy after that, we'll talk. And I'll keep Gerry off your back in the meantime."

"And Drew's back?" Liane asked hopefully.

"Brethren business." Bull wagged a finger at her.

She sighed, and hoped Gerry didn't make Drew's life too miserable. "Understood. I'm fully prepared to ban him from the bar if he gives me shit, though."

"I'm sure that won't be necessary."

Grudgingly, Liane offered a nod. “You’re all right, Bull. I thought, being who you are, you might have tried to push me around, but...”

“It’s never been necessary. You don’t get in my way.”

And with one flat, emotionless glance, he made it very clear that if she did get in his way, he’d run right over her like a steamroller and never look back. But then, she’d been aware of that from the very first moment she came into town. Known that her life hung by a thin thread and that if for even a moment she suspected her cover was compromised, she needed to run and not look back.

There were good reasons that undercover agents were told never to take anything in with them that they couldn’t just walk away from without a backward glance, and to always have multiple alternate bug-out plans.

Which was a point. She needed to check with Drew about his bug-out plans, and revise at least one of hers to make it viable for two people. Liane made a mental note while she smiled mechanically at Bull and slid another beer across the bar for him.

"I appreciate you takin' the time to talk to me. That one's on the house."

The biker nodded at her, scooping the bottle and walking away without further acknowledgment.

A shiver ran down Liane's spine, as though someone had just walked over her grave, but she gave no outward sign, just nodding to a young woman who had been hanging back while Bull was at the bar, beckoning her forward to place her order.

Drew glanced across at her repeatedly, but he didn't come over again, staying in his seat between Bull and Kaleb, perhaps not wanting to antagonize Gerry, who sat and glowered until they finally got up and left. Cash was the one who stopped by to settle the tab, leaving the usual stack of bills on the bar with barely a grunt of acknowledgment to Liane as the others filed out.

Just before five, the throaty roar of a single motorbike reached Liane's ears. Joe, the bartender she employed for busy evenings and when she wanted time off, had already arrived, and the bar was quiet, so she told

Joe to mind the bar for a while and text if he needed her before walking out into the parking lot.

“Hey.” Drew was just removing his helmet, hooking it from his bike’s handlebars, but he paused. “You want to go for a ride?”

“No. Let’s walk.” She nodded towards the trail which ran alongside the creek running behind the roadhouse, a trail which made its way down to Heber’s Lake a half mile distant.

“You got it.” He fell into step beside her, and it was only seconds before they were swallowed up by the trees, the music always blaring from the roadhouse’s speakers fading behind them.

“So,” Drew said after a couple minutes. “You’re ATF?”

“Yes, but never let those letters pass your lips again.” She shot him an admonishing look. “Liane is my real first name, but I’m not telling you my last name - because you don’t need to know.”

“Understood. Well... Drew Murphy is my real name...”

"I know. You're exactly who you say you are. It's just that you thought Jacob was an absolute dickhead, am I right?"

"He was a bullying scumbag when we were kids and he didn't improve with adulthood. Frankly I find it bizarre that he talked about me at all."

"You were just something to brag about. Like having an Olympian or an NFL player in the family."

"You didn't like him either," Drew said astutely.

"He was even worse than Gerry for trying to hit on me. At least Gerry waited until my husband fucked off."

"Was he actually your husband?"

"No, he and the waitress he ran off with were both ATF too. It was all part of the cover story to implant me here. Leaves me as a figure of sympathy, as well as encouraging the Brethren to all want to try and get into my pants and potentially spill secrets while doing so."

"Your bosses didn't encourage you to, ah," he paused delicately.

"Start fucking one of them?" Liane didn't see any point in beating around the bush. "Not something they could order, though they wouldn't have protested if I had. It would have been entirely my choice, if I could stomach any of them, which I couldn't. Which is convenient for you, because it means I'm available for you to start a relationship with."

Chapter Eight

Drew wasn't sure why he'd expected Liane to act differently once they were away from the roadhouse, but she was still just the same; plain-speaking, tough and uncompromising. He watched her from the corner of his eye as they walked along the track together; long legs in skintight jeans, Doc Marten boots on her feet, a black T-shirt faded to gray with the barely-legible logo of a seventies rock band on the front, a khaki overshirt which looked like it was military surplus, sleeves rolled up to her elbows.

He wasn't exactly sure what it was about her that he found so attractive, but discovering she was an ATF agent - totally unexpected as it had been - had actually caused his attraction to increase.

"A relationship?" he echoed.

"Yes. It's the perfect cover for us to share information. I've been told you don't have any direct line to transmit intelligence, other than through me?" She gave him an interrogative look, as they finally reached the lake shoreline.

"Nothing's been set up," he confirmed. "I think, with the earlier leaks, your bosses at... uh, your bosses wanted to minimize the number of people who even know I'm here. So anything I pass to you, you're supposed to make out that it's information you've gathered independently."

Liane nodded, stooping to pick up a stone and skipping it across the water. It skipped three times before sinking into the waves, and she made a face.

"Rubbish," she muttered and chose another stone. "So. What do you have to report?"

"I'm guessing you already know about Kaleb's girlfriend dealing for them at the high school?"

"Yep." She nodded in confirmation. "We didn't pass it on to DEA, though, because frankly we're not talking to them. My boss is convinced that's where the leak is. We're keeping cards close to our chest."

"So you're just going to let a sixteen-year-old girl continue to deal drugs to other high school kids?" Drew couldn't hide the disapproval in his voice.

"It might not seem like it to you, but she's actually the best of a bunch of bad options right now. She appears to have a strong desire not to get caught, and consequently she has a tight leash on her peers. Nobody's allowed to get in too deep, it's cash on the barrel, and if she catches anyone stoned at school, she cuts them off dead."

"A drug dealer with a code?"

"Drugs are being dealt at every high school in America, and if you think they're not, you're being hopelessly naive. Knowing who the dealer is, knowing that her desire not to get caught is overriding her greed and making her work in a tight framework, is as I said... the best of a bunch of bad options."

He didn't like it, but she was right. Picking up a stone of his own, he skimmed it, cursing under his breath as he misjudged the trajectory entirely and it plopped straight into the water.

"What else do you have to report?" Liane watched as he chose another stone and tried again, cocking his head, trying to recalibrate with only one eye.

"Not a lot that you won't already have, unfortunately. I know where most of them live and I'm intimately familiar with all of their bikes, being as they've had me doing scut work like cleaning them and doing basic servicing."

"The problems with being a prospect."

"How long? Even Kaleb won't give me a straight answer." Drew finally managed to get a stone to skip, five times before it sank.

"The last guy before you was six months before they patched him."

"The DEA agent?"

"Yep. And I think they were onto him before they actually patched him. They were just waiting for the right moment to take him out, and patching him made him let his guard down. I didn't get to speak to him before he bugged out, but my boss told me the after-action report said he survived by sheer dumb luck."

"What I heard too." Drew nodded. And then he heard it; the faint crunch of feet on the trail coming down to the lake. "Someone's coming," he said softly.

"It's a popular little walk, unfortunately." Liane made a face, even as she stepped closer to him. "Put your arms around me," she ordered, her voice low.

"I, uh..."

"We're supposed to be literally on a first date, Murphy. Put your arms around me and then you need to kiss me. I don't know if it's one of the Brethren or just someone who might gossip about what they've seen, but either way, word needs to get back that you and I are gettin' busy." She moved right up against him, slipping his arms around her waist.

Drew couldn't help his instinctive reaction, stiffening as she touched him. Awkwardly, he put his arms around her, trying to make them loose so she could easily back away if she wanted.

“Christ, you look as though I’m about to stab you. Try and look like you want this?” Liane said, her eyes searching his face. “Are you okay for this, Murphy? Feels like a role reversal, but I don’t want to push you into anything you don’t want to do.”

“It’s all right,” he muttered, feeling his face flush. “It’s just been a long time since anyone touched me.”

“Ditto,” Liane said, her tone wry, and he remembered that she’d been undercover for over a year.

The sounds he’d heard had gone quiet, and he suspected someone was waiting just inside the tree line, watching them from cover. The hairs on the back of his neck prickled, every sense screaming warning.

“Kiss me if you can,” Liane whispered. “If not, just press your face on my cheek and make it look good.”

She was warm in his arms and softer than she looked, dangerous curves melting against him. It would be all too easy to lose his head, but he was determined not to get pushy. Turning his face against hers, he did as she'd suggested, knowing that to their unseen watcher it would appear as though they kissed passionately.

Liane moved, shifting in his arms, but she was clearly not trying to escape, more acting as though caught in the throes of passion. Finally she pulled her head back slightly and he lifted his, looking down into her eyes. Trying to remember how he should look at a woman after just sharing an intimate kiss.

"It really has been a long time, huh?" Liane said softly.

"I'm sorry. Yeah. Before my last tour started. Not that I was ever any sort of Casanova."

She threw her head back and laughed, but there was nothing mocking in it, again, she was acting. Reaching up, she placed her palm against his cheek, gazing deep into his eyes again, hers a clear, soft blue he almost felt he could drown in.

"I'm sorry it has to be this way," she said quietly, "but I can't think of any other reason for us to regularly talk privately, and even setting up a dead drop to pass notes has its risks."

"Not least that getting time and space to write the notes would be tricky for me at the moment," Drew acknowledged wryly. He was staying over at Kaleb's more often than not, and he doubted Kaleb even had pen and paper in his house. "It's fine. I'm cool with it if you are."

"Sure. But try and get comfortable with casual touches, even if you can't bring yourself to kiss me."

"It's not that I can't bring myself to." Feeling awkward, he dropped his hands, moving back slightly. Trying to put a little space between them before he admitted the truth. "It's that I'm actually really attracted to you. Have been since the first moment I saw you. I don't want to make this awkward by springing a surprise boner on you."

"Oh." Liane looked briefly startled, and then she laughed again, more naturally this time, and surprised him by slipping her hand into his. “Well. Truth be told, I’m not finding this any sort of hardship. In another time, another place… I might well have swiped right on you on Tinder.”

“You’re on Tinder?” Somehow, he couldn’t imagine a woman like Liane needing to resort to online dating. She was gorgeous, with such striking confidence; he couldn’t see that she’d have any shortage of guys asking her out.

“Not in years.” She pulled on his hand, leading him back towards the trail. “I need to get back. The bar’ll be getting busy.”

“Can I help out? Kaleb asked me to be back at his place by nine, but until then, I’m all yours.”

“Yeah, reckon I could use a pair of extra hands, and it looks pretty natural for me to put you to work. I’ll show you the ropes. Ever worked bar before?”

“Nope. I flipped burgers for a while in high school though. I could probably wait tables.”

She considered it before shaking her head. “Reckon Bull will give me shit if I ask you to do that. The Brethren don't wait on nobody. Working bar isn't the same."

"Whatever you think," he said equably, more than happy to let Liane, who knew the territory far better than he, make the call.

There was no sign of anyone else around as they walked back up the trail to the roadhouse, but they still kept the conversation light and chatty, talking about nothing in particular. Liane asked him what music he liked; he asked what her favorite movies were. The kind of things a couple getting to know each other would talk about, if they weren't both undercover agents working hard to put up a front of normality.

The roadhouse was indeed getting busy when they got back, a queue forming at the bar. Liane beckoned Drew to follow her and watch, and leaped into serving drinks with gusto.

"Brethren working behind the bar now?" one guy asked, eying his cut as Drew set his beer on the counter.

"Y'all got something to say about that?" Drew growled.

"No!" The guy shook his head vigorously. "Good to see y'all gainfully employed, that's all. Not that you're not otherwise, ah, gainfully employed!"

Drew offered a dangerous glare in response, and the guy, who apparently had more hair than common sense, hastily slapped a ten on the counter and fled with his beer in hand.

"Try not to scare the customers," Liane said as she passed, and gave his ass a quick slap, making him jump. "I'd say he's a big softy really, but it'd be a massive lie," she commented loudly, making a few customers close enough to hear chuckle.

"Looks pretty hard to me," a woman waiting for her drinks answered, running her eyes over Drew's physique. "If Gerry had a body like that, I might not mind so much when he kept patting my ass!"

Liane smirked. "Behave yourself, Maura. Drew's spoken for."

"Shame," Maura murmured, but she smiled at Liane. "No harm in window shopping?"

"No law against it." Liane shrugged, and deliberately grazed the whole length of her body against Drew as she passed. Determined to get comfortable with the casual contact, he forced himself not to flinch, just reaching out to put a hand on her waist briefly as she paused beside him.

For just a moment, as she looked up at him, the noisy bar around them faded away. His gaze fell to her lips, soft and plush, slightly parted, and he very nearly just leaned down and kissed her.

And then someone banged on the bar and the moment was broken. Drew jerked his gaze away from Liane, aware he was flushing, grateful the lights in the bar were pretty low.

Her fingers ghosted lightly over his arm before she moved away, going to take another order.

This is going to be complicated. Sustaining a fake relationship at the same time as keeping the Brethren convinced that I'm a white supremacist with no moral compass.

On the other hand, having someone he could actually let his guard down around might be invaluable. He was already starting to feel the strain of being permanently ‘on’ after only a few weeks. He couldn’t begin to imagine how Liane had sustained it for over a year thus far. Maybe even more; it was possible she’d spent her entire ATF career to date under cover in different situations.

Glancing at Liane as she deftly mixed a pitcher of margaritas for Maura and her friends, Drew wondered how old Liane was. Her colorful pixie-styled hair made her look younger than he suspected she really was. She could pass for early twenties, but he reckoned she was probably closer to his own age of thirty-one.

The roadhouse was busy, two servers taking orders and running meals from the kitchen, Drew helping out Liane and Joe behind the bar. The next couple of hours passed quickly, though he kept an eye on the time. He didn’t know if Kaleb would report back to Bull if Drew didn’t get in by nine, and he didn’t want to test it out.

“I’m gonna have to head out,” he said to Liane finally.

She took a quick glance around. "I'll walk you out."

Things were starting to quieten down; the kitchen had sent out the last meals a little while before, and most folks who'd just come to eat had now left. Joe nodded when Liane asked him to hold the fort for five minutes.

"I didn't get the opportunity to tell you earlier," Liane said quietly as they stood in the car park beside his bike, "but there are microphones installed here with a feed going back to HQ. One at the Brethren's usual table and one in this tree by where the bikes are parked. So if you get the opportunity to encourage any indiscreet talk in those locations, please do."

"Understood." Conscious of people moving around in the car park, any of whom might well happily answer questions for the Brethren if asked, Drew held out his arms. Liane stepped into them willingly, reaching up to slip her own around his neck.

"Come to terms with the idea of kissing me yet?"

"It's not something I ever had any objection to, I just want to make that clear!"

She laughed softly, and then her hand exerted gentle pressure on the back of his neck, pulling his face down towards hers.

Well, here goes.

He kissed her.

Chapter Nine

Liane truly hadn't expected Drew to kiss quite so well. His lips were warm and firm, lower lip dragging slightly against hers with a delicious friction which had her opening her mouth without even intending to.

She felt Drew stiffen with surprise, and then he seemed to relax into the kiss. His tongue stroked over hers, lightly teasing, and she shivered with a sudden shock of desire.

"This could get complicated." Drew pulled back and whispered it against her lips.

"My life is the definition of complicated, what do you mean, it could get complicated?"

He let out a low, husky laugh before pulling back. "I need to go." Callused fingertips traced the curve of her jaw gently. “The gang are all coming in for lunch tomorrow, so I’ll see you then.”

“Bring me in as much as you can. I’m a woman so membership isn’t going to be an option, but being an old lady is the next best thing. I’m going to make out like I’m blinded by lust; you play it a bit cooler. If Bull thinks I’m chasing after you he may try to push the envelope with me, see how much business he can get away with doing at the roadhouse.”

“Every instinct is screaming at me to keep you far away from them.” Drew gave her a rueful grin. “Caveman instincts trying to kick in, I’m sorry.”

“Because I’m a woman?”

He nodded. “It’s not that I don’t believe you’re perfectly capable, and certainly far better trained than I am for this sort of undercover work. It’s just instincts.”

“Try and stomp on them. We’re working together, and you’re not my bodyguard. Your job here isn’t to protect me; it’s to gather intelligence.”

"I know." He leaned his brow against hers. "I have the feeling it's going to take everything we've both got to get this mission done. I'm not going to be stupid enough to try to cut you out of anything in the mistaken belief I'm protecting you."

"See that you don't." Liane found herself smiling, though. He was so sincere. So honest. Fear crawled through her; how could this man survive the necessary life of lies which was undercover work? Surely, he would slip up.

On the other hand, she thought as she watched him mount his Harley and ride away, his undercover legend was basically his real identity. The only thing he was lying about was his beliefs.

Unlike her. She smiled to herself as she turned around and looked at the roadhouse, listened to the rock music blasting from inside. It was a long, long way from the exclusive little Virginia town where Liane Hagerty had grown up, daughter of two DC lobbyists who had spoiled their three daughters rotten, sending them to expensive private schools and funding every hobby they took it into their heads to try out.

Middle child Liane had been the sporty one, her youngest sister Jessikah was a tech genius who owned every gadget ever created - and had invented a few herself - and the eldest daughter, Kelsey, was the beauty of the family, the kind of girl who made heads turn wherever she went. She started modeling at the age of thirteen and five years later was making more than both her parents combined, traveling internationally to film commercials and walk runways for major fashion designers.

Liane shut her eyes against the sting of tears, remembering the last time she'd seen Kelsey. At New York Fashion Week, just after walking the runway in a glorious couture designer gown. The Hagerty family had taken a trip to New York so they could get to see Kelsey's triumph in person, for once. At a celebratory dinner afterwards, Liane had followed Kelsey into the bathroom and caught her sister snorting cocaine off the marble vanity.

"How the hell do you think I stay this thin?" Kelsey had snapped when Liane had confronted her. “An extra pound and work starts drying up pretty damn quick. The coke keeps my metabolism running fast enough I don’t have to starve.”

“Do Mom and Dad know?”

“Of course not, and don’t you dare tell them.” Kelsey’s eyes were dark, glittering dangerously. “I know what I’m doing.”

Only fifteen, Liane hadn’t known what to do. She’d kept quiet that evening, and lain awake all night in the hotel, wrestling with her conscience.

The following morning, a knock on the hotel door proved to be the police. Kelsey had gone to see her dealer after dinner, apparently to buy more cocaine. She’d walked straight into the middle of a turf war. A stray round had hit her in the stomach and she bled to death before paramedics arrived.

From that moment forward, Liane’s path had been set. She was going into law enforcement. A master’s in criminology and she applied to all the major federal agencies. ATF had been quick to snap her up.

She'd been singled out for undercover work from the beginning. She was a good natural actress and with the right haircut, makeup and clothes, could look either significantly younger or older than her years. The last eight years since joining the agency had been spent almost entirely undercover; very few of her fellow ATF agents would even know her by sight. Her work had put dozens, maybe hundreds, of criminals behind bars. Kept even more guns off the streets and doubtlessly saved countless lives.

This assignment had been her longest yet, though. Well over a year in the back end of nowhere, getting nowhere fast with the investigation, and she was tired and beginning to think that her days as an undercover agent might be numbered. Liane wanted to be herself again… if she even knew who that was, after so long pretending to be someone else.

“I'm gonna get these guys, Kels,” Liane whispered to the night sky. “I'm gonna get them, and then… I'm gonna go figure out who I am now.”

It was almost fifteen years since that stray bullet had stolen Kelsey's life. Almost half of Liane's life. Kelsey's death had changed the whole family; her parents' marriage had collapsed within a few months, their father quickly remarrying and soon accepting a post with the State Department which saw him posted all over the world. Liane could count on one hand the number of times she'd seen him since her high school graduation.

Their mother had fallen into herself. The formerly confident lobbyist had dissolved into a bundle of anxiety and nerves, barely able to get through every day. Years of medication and therapy later, she had reinvented herself entirely as a yoga instructor and now lived and worked at a rehab center for the rich and famous - including some of the politicians with whom she'd once worked.

Jessikah had wanted to go into law enforcement too, but she'd chosen a different path. Brilliant with computers, she'd been recruited right out of college by the NSA. Three years ago, though, she'd announced she was leaving the agency and joining a private security group. She was actually more secretive now she was in the private sector than when she'd been working for the government.

Liane missed Jessikah most of all, and as she stood alone outside the roadhouse, reluctant to go back in and immerse herself once again in the grind of her undercover persona, she resolved that when this assignment was done, she was going to find her sister and spend some quality time with her. Get to know who Jessikah was now and what she was doing with her life.

Maybe Liane would even have the time to explore a relationship.

She laughed quietly to herself, thinking that Drew's kiss really must have had quite an effect. She was thinking about stuff which hadn't crossed her mind in years.

A shout from inside the roadhouse made her square her shoulders and shake off her sudden melancholy. There was work to be done, and nobody else was going to do it. She needed to get through the rest of the evening, clean up, and once she was alone in her apartment, log on and report to her handler that she'd made contract with Drew and they were going to conduct a fake relationship in order to give him good cover to regularly report intelligence to her. She'd pass on the few small snippets he'd been able to give her, none of which were new, but all corroborated things she'd already reported.

And this time, she'd hope they decided to do something about that damned girl dealing drugs at the high school.

That said, she didn't even know if the ATF had shared that information with the DEA. After realizing there was a leak somewhere, the three agencies had stopped talking to each other about this case. Trust was at an all-time low.

A car pulled into the lot, beams raking over Liane briefly, and she saw the blue-and-white paint, the light bar on the top. A vehicle from the sheriff's department.

Suddenly, she knew how to deal with the girl. Sheriff Hunter hadn't been in his post long, but he was obviously a straight shooter, and there was no way he would tolerate a student dealing drugs at a school in his district if he knew about it.

Now, she just needed to figure out how to get the anonymous tip into Hunter's ear. It wasn't him getting out of the car, but he did stop into the roadhouse at least once a week. He'd even brought his girlfriend in to eat, and they'd both praised the food.

And just like that, she knew how to get to Jason Hunter. His girlfriend was a lawyer in Woodvale, the next town over from Redstone Creek. She must have an address, probably easily findable on the internet. Liane could write an anonymous tip, sign it 'a federal agent undercover in Redstone Creek' and drop it in the mail to her.

Satisfied with the plan, she opened the door to the roadhouse and gestured politely for the sheriff's deputy who'd just arrived to go in ahead of her. She couldn't remember the guy's name; another of the new deputies Hunter had recruited when half the department had ended up arrested or fired for collusion with the Manhunters.

"Evening," she said cheerfully.

"Busy night?" the deputy asked.

"Not particularly. Just been out to get a breath of air. Kitchen's finished and it's a week night; folks will be heading home soon. Get some sleep before work tomorrow."

The deputy nodded. "Any trouble with the Brethren?" he asked, apparently casually.

"I don't give them no trouble, they don't give me none." Deliberately, Liane turned to give him her back, indicating she wasn't going to discuss the Brethren with him. They were inside the roadhouse now and while none of the gang were in, Liane could see at least three women she knew had been involved with members at one time or another. One who was still on and off with Gerry, whenever she was drunk enough. It would only take a few words from one of them that Liane was talking to the sheriff's department about the Brethren's business, and any trust they had in her would be gone completely.

"Have any of them been in today?" the deputy persisted, following her to the bar.

"I don't keep a register of who comes in and out of my bar, Deputy." Turning to face him, she raised a brow. "Now, are you on or off duty?"

"Off." He looked puzzled.

"Then I suggest you sit your ass down and order a drink, or my customers are going to think you'll be watching them out the door and picking who to pin a DUI on."

His eyes widened. And then he sat meekly down on a stool and asked for a Bud Light.

She was sure she heard him mutter "Hardass," into his beer. Which frankly, she didn't mind at all. His presence was definitely depressing the mood in the bar, folks settling their tabs and shrugging on their coats, heading for the door quickly, hoping to be long gone by the time he finished his beer and headed out. Not great for business, but Liane couldn't bring herself to care. With any luck, the place would be empty before closing time and she could get a rare early night.

Chapter Ten

"You done?"

Drew sighed at the question, pushed with his feet on the ground to slide the creeper trolley out from under Bull's truck, and frowned up at Kaleb. "I'll be done a lot quicker if you don't keep asking me if I'm done every five minutes."

"We're going to the roadhouse for lunch. C'mon, we can come back and finish this later. Bull doesn't need the truck for a couple more days, he said so."

"I don't much like leaving a job half done. Shouldn't take much longer."

"C'mon, I'm hungry!"

Drew half-laughed, pushing himself upright and reaching for a rag to wipe his oily hands. “You can’t still be growing.”

Kaleb grinned back at him. “Maybe.”

“Alright, alright. Guess I’m hungry too.”

“And you can see your old lady.” Kaleb nudged him slyly in the ribs as they went to the sink at the back of Bull’s garage to wash up. “Two weeks is up tomorrow. You gonna ask Bull if you can pursue a relationship with her?”

Drew shrugged, affecting nonchalance. From the corner of his eye, he’d spotted Bull standing just on the other side of the open connecting door to the house, listening to them talk. “I guess. My type usually runs more to busty blondes in short skirts and cowboy boots. Never had a woman who gives me so much back talk, either.”

“But you like her?” Kaleb persisted.

“I like her well enough. And I’m not about to turn down a free fuck. Spent too many nights with only my right hand for company.” He gave Kaleb a wry look. “Being on deployment to third world hellholes sucks balls.”

“Long as you don’t have to suck balls!” Kaleb laughed crudely and slapped his shoulder, and then lowered his voice, surprising Drew. “I just wanted to warn you. Gerry was obvious about pursuing Liane and has been blatantly pissy about you getting with her, but Bull had his eye on her too.”

And Bull can hear every word of this conversation. Drew thought very fast.

“I don’t want to step on any toes. Should I bow out?”

“Nah, don’t reckon so.” Kaleb shrugged. “If Bull wants her bad enough, he’ll tell you to step off and take his shot. But Liane picked you, didn’t she? Made it pretty clear she liked you from early on.”

“She’s not a woman who’s shy about going after what she wants,” Drew agreed. “Don’t know why she picked me, to be honest. Maybe it’s just that I’m her type.”

“You don’t look much like her ex-husband,” Kaleb said consideringly, “but I guess he was tall and athletic too. And clean-shaven.”

Unlike Bull and Gerry, who were both of average height, thick-bodied and bearded. Drew had the rangy, lean build common to Special Forces soldiers, muscled but capable of running long distances carrying a full pack of gear. And he’d spent enough time on long deployments being unable to shave and hating the itchy feeling of it. He never went more than a couple of days without taking the razor to his face now.

“Look, I’m acting cool about it, but she’s a good woman,” he said. “And a businesswoman, at that. Gotta respect a woman who works hard and is making a success out of her business. I like that about her very much.”

“The roadhouse is a hell of an asset,” Kaleb said, as they walked back out of the garage, pulling the door down behind them, and went to their bikes. “Maybe if you’re dating her, she’ll be a bit more lax with us, hey? Look the other way if we need to do business there.”

"Softly, softly," Drew shot him a grin. "Let me work up to that. I don't want to get dumped before we've hardly had time to get started."

Kaleb headed over to knock on the house door, and Bull came out a couple of minutes later, shrugging into his jacket.

"You got that oil change done?" he grunted, buckling his helmet on.

"Just about. We'll finish it up this afternoon," Drew said.

"See that you do." And then Bull kicked his bike's engine into life and there was no more opportunity for talking.

They followed the same routine they'd followed every couple of days for the past two weeks, cruising around town to pick everyone up, until the Brethren was at full strength, with the sole exception of Gerry. They never went to Gerry's place; Drew had no idea where it was, but assumed he lived out of town somewhere. The sergeant-at-arms was always waiting for them at the junction out to the highway, cruising with them the last couple of miles down to the roadhouse.

Drew wasn't sure if it was wishful thinking on his part or just good acting on hers, but Liane's eyes seemed to brighten as he strode into the roadhouse, at the tail of the gang as befitted his prospective status. She certainly turned up the wattage on her smile for him, even though she greeted Bull first, polite without being deferential.

"Busy in here today." Bull grunted, looking around.

"Summer's coming," Liane agreed. "Folks starting to come out to spend weekends at the lake."

"Hm." Bull didn't look particularly pleased about that, but then, he never looked pleased by anything so far as Drew could tell.

"Of course, your table's reserved for you."

"Damn right," Gerry grunted, pushing past a group of people waiting at the bar, one of whom turned around, possibly to make an angry retort, which died on his lips as the burly, leather-clad biker glared at him. "What are you looking at?" Gerry growled.

The guy looked terrified, licked his lips. “Nothing!”

“Think I’m nothing, do you?”

“No! I - was just - looking for a vacant table!”

“Don’t play with the kid, Gerry.” Cash pushed Gerry in the back. “No trouble. We’re here to eat.”

“Humph.” Gerry glared a for a few seconds longer but the kid was already staring fixedly at the floor, pale-faced.

“Hey, you.” Liane nudged Drew lightly on the arm.

“Hey.” He leaned down to kiss her, just a brief brush of lips.

She smiled up at him, and murmured, loud enough for Bull standing nearby to hear, “And that’s why I’d never date Gerry. He likes to scare my customers. It’s terrible for business.”

“Looks like business is pretty good today,” Drew noted.

“Sure is. If you got some time after you’ve finished eating, we could maybe go out for a while.”

“Like a date?” He grinned.

“Or what passes for one, in this town. I want to go to the range. Thought you could give me a ride on that bike of yours.”

“The shooting range?” His brows shot up.

“That woman of yours is a good shot,” Bull said, obviously uncaring that he’d just given away that he was eavesdropping on their conversation. “I’ve seen her at the range.”

“This bar can get pretty rowdy. Folks behave themselves a lot better when they know I’ve got a sawn-off under the bar and I’m a crack shot with a pistol.” Liane grinned, showing her teeth. “Haven’t been to the range in a while, though.”

“I’m supposed to be finishing an oil change on Bull’s truck,” Drew said, glancing sideways at Bull. The club president considered briefly before nodding.

“I appreciate your dedication. Saturday, I’ve got an errand for you to run in it. As long as it's done by then, I don't mind. So take the afternoon with your old lady, if you want."

"Old lady, am I?" Liane said. "Does that mean we're official?"

"If you want to be. Drew's shown good loyalty to us so far and I think you could be an asset to the club."

"My rules..."

"We'll discuss those at a later time. Maybe outside opening hours, when there's less ears around to eavesdrop on what ain't their business."

Liane tilted her head, staring at Bull consideringly, and then she looked at Drew, allowing her expression to visibly soften. Playing the besotted girlfriend, he thought, in awe of her acting skills.

"All right," she said. "I can't let my liquor license be put at risk, but... all right. We'll talk."

"Good girl," Bull said, and then he gave Drew's shoulder an approving squeeze and walked past him, heading for their table. "Get the first round of beers in," he instructed over his shoulder.

Liane put nine beer bottles and a Coke onto a tray and watched as Drew picked it up and made his way across the bar to the Brethren's table. He delivered Bull's beer first and then worked his way around the table, serving everyone else before taking his own seat, like a good little prospect, in between Kaleb and Cash. Kaleb said something, which made Drew smile and glance up at her, and Gerry scowl from his place at the other end of the table. Maybe Bull had told the others that he'd given Drew the green light to have a proper relationship with her.

It wasn't even real, but something inside Liane still warmed at the thought. Permission meant Drew could stay overnight. Meant they could go on dates.

"I really thought you were smarter than to get involved with one of them," a voice said, and she scowled at Merrick, the waiter, as he picked up a pitcher of beers for one of the other tables.

"I ain't paying you to judge me, kiddo. Keep your opinions to yourself. Be better for your health, anyway." She wasn't kidding about that last. Nobody in Redstone Creek who had any sense did any shit-talking about the Brethren.

Merrick just huffed as he walked away. Liane kept the smile from her face. He was a good kid. Deserved better than a life waiting tables in this dead-end town. He was saving for tuition to go to college in the fall; she'd write him a damn good reference and hopefully he'd be able to get another job to support himself while he studied. In fact, she thought privately, she should write that reference now and give it to her boss, to post to Merrick in case she had to bail early and without notice. With any luck, the job would be wrapped up and she'd no longer be here by the fall anyway.

The lunch rush quieted down, folks filtering out, and Drew lingered behind when the rest of the Brethren left, giving Merrick a hand to clear tables, even though the kid gave him the stink eye for it. Which disappeared when Drew handed him a small pile of bills.

"I found these under plates. Your tips."

Merrick muttered an ungracious thanks as he took the money, but Liane saw his startled sideways glance as he scurried into the kitchen.

"A real biker wouldn't have given him the money," she murmured to Drew, walking up beside him.

"They were his tips." Drew's brow furrowed. "He works his ass off for them. Why should I get the money, just for picking up a few plates?"

"Your sense of honor is showing. Just saying. Kaleb or Cash or Gerry would have pocketed it without a second thought. Merrick's now thinking that you don't add up."

"Oh." Drew grimaced. "Blowing my cover?" His voice was very soft; they were the only ones in the room now anyway.

"No. He doesn't like the Brethren anyway, so he's not going to blab, but just be careful. You're not acting ruthless enough."

"Noted." He didn't look particularly happy at the idea. Up close and personal being an asshole was going to be tricky for him, Liane thought, but he was going to have to get his hands at least a little dirty while he was undercover.

"You ready to go? I just need to pick up my gun and some ammunition."

"Sure. Do you have a helmet? Bull says we gotta make sure to obey the road rules. Don't give the sheriff's department an excuse." They shared a glance of amusement.

"I do, actually. It's upstairs. Give me five minutes. I want a clean shirt, too." As usual, the one she was currently wearing had come in for its fair share of beer spills as she worked the busy bar.

"I'll wait on you outside?" He glanced at the bar. "Or do you want me to mind in here?"

Joey pushed his way in through the outside door at that moment, greeting them both with a nod and a grunt, and Liane shook her head.

"Nah, Joey's got it. See you outside in five."

Drew was leaning against his bike when she came down, and she paused a moment, unseen, to just admire him. He did look good leaning on that Harley. If you could ignore the gang insignia on his leather vest, anyway.

“Hey.” He straightened up as she approached, eyes raking her up and down in a bold appraisal she surprisingly found she didn’t mind at all, from him. His right eye wasn’t tracking the same as his left, she noted.

“How’s your shooting, with that eye?” she asked.

Drew’s expression shuttered instantly. “Shit,” he muttered, turning away from her to sling a leg across his bike. “My depth perception’s fucked all to hell. I used to be able to hit a quarter at half a mile; now I’d be lucky to hit a car at that range.”

That had to be tough, for a former elite sniper. Liane sympathized, but she still asked “That’s with your rifle. What about a pistol?”

He glanced back at her as she mounted behind him, surprise clear on his face. “I don’t have one. Haven’t fired one in a while.”

“You’re not carrying?” That startled her. Idaho was a pretty lax state as far as gun laws went;

open carry was legal with a license, and they weren't hard to get. She was pretty sure the rest of the Brethren all carried guns all the time.

"No."

"Then you're a fool. Our line of work, there's all too likely going to come a time when it's going to come down to guns. If you don't have one, you're not even in the fight."

"What if I can't hit the side of a fucking barn with it?"

He sounded bitter as hell. Liane put her arms around his waist and her chin on his shoulder, spoke directly into his ear. "I call bullshit, soldier. You don't need two eyes to hit a bad guy standing right in front of you. Take me to the range, and we're getting you a damn handgun."

She felt rather than heard a chuckle run through his frame, and then he put one hand on hers briefly before setting them both on the handlebars and starting the bike. The engine's throaty roar put paid to any further conversation, for now at least.

Chapter Eleven

The range was attached to a local sporting goods store, or primarily a gun store, Drew saw as they walked inside. The ratty-faced guy behind the counter was a face he knew. One he'd seen at Cash's place several times, though they'd never been introduced. As far as he knew, Rat-face wasn't a member of the Brethren - but then, quite probably, being a member of an outlaw motorcycle gang was the kind of thing that would get your license to sell firearms revoked pretty damned fast.

"Shooting today, Liane?" Rat-face asked.

"Hey, Bobby. Yup. Give me two boxes of the usual. And Drew here needs a piece."

Bobby snapped the gum he was chewing, gestured grandiosely towards the glass case behind the counter. “Take your pick, man. I know Cash’ll settle up for you later.”

“Generous,” Drew murmured under his breath, surveying the array of handguns. “Don’t need anything too fancy.”

“What about a nice basic Glock 19?” Liane suggested.

“Sure.” He didn’t really care. It wasn’t like his beloved rifle, locked up safely in the gun safe which was the only thing he’d installed in his cousin’s cabin.

Bobby put the gun on the counter and Drew checked it by reflex, disassembling and reassembling it in a few quick, practiced moves.

“Heard ya was Special Forces.” There was nothing but respect in Bobby’s tone.

“Rangers.” The clip was empty, of course. Drew picked up two of the four boxes of 9mm Parabellum rounds Bobby set on the counter next. “Thanks.”

“You got it.” Bobby shook his head when Liane took out her credit card. “I’ll put yours on the Brethren's tab." He winked at her. "Since you're Drew's old lady now and all."

"News travels fast," she murmured, glancing sideways at Drew as she opened the door leading through to the range. "Didn't think Bobby was Brethren."

"I think he can't be, officially, but unofficially? In it up to his neck. I don't know that there's a group chat or anything - I haven't been invited to one - but I think he and Cash are pretty tight."

"Cash's old lady is Bobby's cousin," Liane advised softly.

"Ah." That made sense.

There was nobody else on the range, at the moment. There was no range safety officer; Bobby came through from the shop and asked them both to sign waivers, before gesturing at a pile of earmuffs and eye glasses and telling them to use what they wanted. Liane was obviously used to the place, picking up a pile of paper targets and heading downrange with them, hanging one up in each of the six shooting lanes.

Drew took the time to load the Glock's magazine, getting used to the feel of the small, stubby nine millimeter cartridges again after a long time in which he hadn't handled anything but his rifle rounds. I'm being an ammo snob, he thought with an amused grin at himself, before his grin faded.

Twenty yards. It's nothing. He'd aced all his firearms training in the Rangers, had regularly shot all kinds of weapons to ensure he kept in practice.

And right now, he wasn't sure he could hit a paper target more than a foot across, at twenty yards. Never mind hit the bullseye.

Liane didn't say anything when she came back to his side. Just unzipped her jacket, reached inside and drew a gun from an underarm holster.

Drew had expected her to have a Glock 19M, standard issue for ATF agents, and that was exactly what she pulled out and laid on the counter, but... it was pink.

"Pink," he said in disbelief.

Liane winked at him. "Pretty, isn't it?"

Nobody would ever suspect a federal agent to be waving around a pink handgun. He almost laughed.

Liane loaded her gun with quick, efficient movements, though he suspected she was actually being deliberately a little sloppy. Bobby had gone back to the shop counter, but there were cameras in the range. Who knew who might be watching them? A woman being competent with a gum wasn't unusual. One who was using classical 'law enforcement' movements, stance and tactics? That might ring alarm bells in someone's mind.

Because Drew knew what he was looking for, he saw Liane deliberately relax her stance, go sloppy, after she stepped up to the firing line. She fired off a full clip, fifteen rounds, in a steady rhythm: single shots, letting her hand come back down after each recoil, re-sighting methodically before firing again.

She was hitting the target, but in inconsistent groupings, never in the X-ring. He suspected she was deliberately throwing her aim off very slightly, not wanting to appear too good for whoever was watching; just good enough to appear competent and dangerous, not good enough to look well-trained.

When she reached the end of the magazine, she ejected it and laid the gun down on the counter before turning to Drew, her blue eyes steady behind the clear plastic safety glasses. "Next target's yours."

"I don't..." he trailed off. "I don't know if I can hit it," he said quietly after a moment.

"I don't give a fuck if you think you can hit it right now, by the time we leave here you will be able to."

Drew felt his eyes go wide with shock as Liane stepped in closer and spoke, her voice low and intense.

"You are my backup here, Drew Murphy. If the shit hits the fan, I need you to have my back. Including shooting people off it, if it comes down to that. You don't need two eyes to shoot a damn pistol, so pick that gun up and start shooting."

Drew's hands were moving before she'd even finished speaking. "You sound like my old drill sergeant from my days back in Basic," he groused, though it was ridiculous to compare the two. Sergeant Diaz would have made two of Liane. The tone was the same, though; calm, absolutely unshakable in the confidence that orders would be obeyed. Sergeant Diaz had never needed to shout to get his point across, and Liane didn't either.

"I don't care if we go through these four entire boxes of ammunition," Liane said quietly as he slotted the loaded clip into his gun, his hands shaking slightly with nerves. "I don't care if we have to go and buy four more boxes. Or eight. You're going to get this, Drew. We just have to retrain your reflexes."

It wasn't going to take four boxes, Liane saw when he started to shoot. Yes, he was missing a few here and there, but not by a lot. Once he closed his bad eye and started to focus, he improved dramatically, too. She leaned on the counter and watched in silence. Undoubtedly he had many more hours of range time than her; it would be insulting for her to offer him tips. He'd figure it out himself.

Even if it took four boxes.

Drew put three clips' worth into the first target before moving on to the second, and immediately, Liane could see he'd figured it out. He didn't miss the target at all this time. And by the time he got to the last target, all the holes were clustered in a tight grouping no bigger than her hand.

She saw his shoulders slump as he safed the gun and set it down on the counter, and then he turned to her, a smile lifting the corners of his mouth.

"Thank you. Clearly, what I needed was someone to kick my ass."

"You'd lost your nerve. It can happen to anyone," she said gently. "Losing the sight in that eye is a hell of a thing to get past. But if you tell yourself you can't, you never will. You've lost the battle before you even start."

"Is that how you get through... doing what you do?"

“Self-belief? It’s the only way to survive my line of work.” They’d both pushed their ear protectors down around their necks, were talking quietly, nose to nose. It’d look like an intimate conversation between lovers, to anyone watching on the cameras. “I’ve made a difference. Done things nobody else, outside the situation, could have handled. And I will again.” Gently, she poked the middle of his chest with a finger. “So will you.”

There was a brief moment of electric silence. Drew reached up, curled his fingers around hers. Lifted them to his mouth and kissed her fingertips lightly.

Liane took a deep, slow breath. Mentally weighed up pros and cons.

The scale came down heavily on the side of the pros.

“We should go back to my place.”

Drew’s eyebrows flew up. “To... talk?”

“We can do that, sure. I was hoping you’d be open to more, though.”

“Is that...” he paused, seemed to sort through and discard several different words before selecting the ones he wanted, "personal preference?"

"Yes." She grinned up at him. "There are no rules against it, if that's what you're asking. Nor am I under orders to seduce you or anything like that. Getting to let my guard down with someone is a rarity. Getting to do it with someone I'd have been very attracted to if I met them in anything remotely resembling our real lives? Vanishingly unlikely. You can say no, of course... but I think we could both do with blowing off some steam."

"That's what it'd be... just a release of mutual tension?"

"If that's what you want to call it, sure." Liane shrugged, ignoring an annoying little voice somewhere in the back of her mind which was whispering about emotional involvement. "I can't promise white picket fences. Neither can you. It's very probable we'll never see each other again when this is all over."

"Understood." He looked deep into her eyes, and then seemed to come to a decision. "Just so you know. If this was anything resembling our real lives… I'd probably be thinking hopefully about those picket fences. But since it's not, I'm more than happy to take you up on your offer."

The little voice inside her head was getting louder, but Liane determinedly ignored it. Standing on tiptoe, she curled an arm around Drew's neck, pulling him down towards her.

This kiss wasn't for show. Wasn't practice. Wasn't tentative. It was deep and hungry from the start, two people with no outlet for deeply buried passions finding freedom in each other.

Drew made a muffled sound against her lips, but it wasn't protest, because when she pulled back to look at him, he shook his head and hauled her back in again. Growling her name under his breath.

It had been a long, long time since a man's kiss had made Liane's toes curl, had made her belly clench with excitement. For a brief moment she forgot where they were, forgot everything except the heat of Drew's mouth against hers, the lean solidity of his body as her hands roamed over his chest.

And then her fingers found the edge of his leather vest and she flinched back.

"I want to get this off," Drew said, low and urgent. "It's not who I am."

"I know." And she did; the vest to him was like a uniform, and he had to behave a specific way, play his part while he was wearing it. "My place."

"Yes."

They gathered up their guns and the unused rounds, cleaned up their spent brass, threw out the perforated targets without really speaking much, just working efficiently, needing to get out of there as quickly as possible. Drew did pause in the shop on the way out to gruffly thank Bobby and select an underarm holster for his new gun, taking his cut off briefly to fit the holster tight to his body.

"It's not exactly quick draw, but I'm damned if I'll shove the bloody thing in my pants and shoot myself in the ass," Drew muttered as he rebuttoned the cut and patted his sides, checking that the gun didn't appear overly obtrusive.

Liane covered her mouth, trying not to laugh at the image his words evoked. He was referring to Gerry, she knew, who did indeed always have his gun shoved into the back of his pants, often easily visible as he moved. She'd been tempted so many times to just steal it, but Gerry wasn't the kind of guy it was smart to play pranks on. He'd probably have thought she was trying to flirt with him.

Chapter Twelve

The ride back to the roadhouse took them past the high school, where Liane noticed a couple of vehicles from the sheriff's department parked outside the gates and a pretty blonde in a cheerleader's uniform being perp-walked out in cuffs. She hid a smile against Drew's back as they roared past.

"Was that who I think it was, getting arrested?" Drew asked as they parked up the bike and headed up to her apartment above the roadhouse.

"I don't know who you could be referring to," Liane said virtuously, and entirely untruthfully.

Drew eyed her cynically. She offered an innocent smile.

"Hm." He fished out his phone. "I better call it in. Otherwise word might get back that I rode past, and then I'll be asked why I didn't call it in."

"Of course." She pulled out her keys, unlocked the door to her apartment. Drew looked at the heavy door with the three separate deadlocks with raised brows, but made no comment.

She was a single woman living in an apartment over a roadhouse. It was perfectly logical for her to take her personal security seriously.

Gesturing Drew to the couch, she headed to her kitchen to start the coffee machine. While she didn't need to be back down at the bar until six or so, it would be a long evening after that. She'd need coffee to get her through.

"Yeah, I'm pretty sure it was Kaleb's girl," she heard Drew say behind her. "Sheriff's department. No, I didn't see anything that looked like a Fed car. How would I know? Girl's a cheerleader. Of course she's got enemies. One of them probably ratted on her."

Well, it could indeed have been some nerdy kid the pretty cheerleader and her friends had picked on, Liane thought. That was a perfectly viable explanation.

"I don't bloody know. Ask her, or get your lawyer to ask her! Probably some boy who wanted to take her to a dance and she shot him down! Who the hell knows?" Drew's voice rose with irritation. "I called you because I thought you might want to tell Kaleb yourself. Do you want me to come in?"

He obviously received an answer in the negative, because his voice quieted, and by the time Liane had poured two cups of coffee, he'd finished the call and come to stand in the kitchen doorway, watching her.

He'd lost no time in stripping off the cut, Liane saw as she turned to face him, removing the gun and holster too. His black T-shirt clung lovingly to his lean, solid frame, biceps bulging thickly from the sleeves.

"Coffee?" she asked, knowing she was eating him up with her eyes. Knowing he saw it.

"Not bothered, to be honest." He walked toward her in an easy prowl.

Liane licked her lips.

“I was pretty sure you were inviting me back here for something other than coffee.” He hooked his thumbs in his belt loops, stilling, waiting. Waiting for her to make the first move.

His patience was one of the sexiest damn things about him, Liane acknowledged to herself. So many men were grabby, or thought when you gave an inch it was an invitation to take a mile. Maybe it was his sniper training. All those endless hours of waiting. He looked like he was perfectly prepared to turn around and leave if she said she’d changed her mind.

She was most definitely not changing her mind. They might not get anything more than these few stolen moments, but she was going to take them and be grateful. Reaching out, she grabbed a double fistful of his shirt and yanked up.

Drew took the hint instantly, whipping the shirt off over his head and discarding it.

Well, he certainly hadn’t let himself go to seed since his medical discharge from the Rangers.

If there was a spare ounce of fat on him, she couldn't see it. He was lean and hard, dark hair curling on his chest and down in a thin happy trail arrowing to his waistband.

She'd been with guys who were gym fit. A couple of her fellow agents who kept themselves in shape. But not like this, not Special Forces fit. She reached out to touch him almost wonderingly, tracing the eight-pack - eight-pack! - of perfectly chiselled abs.

A warm hand came up to catch hers, pressing it against his skin, and then his other arm snaked around her.

"Your confidence is so damn sexy," Drew said, his voice low and rough. "I couldn't take my eyes off you even before I knew we were on the same side."

"Same," she admitted, and then she reached up and kissed him.

With his shirt off, she could explore that whole delicious torso with her hands while their tongues dueled, light at first and then deeper, hungrier.

Drew made a fierce sound in his throat and suddenly his hands curled under her ass and he lifted, putting her on the countertop, which put their mouths at exactly the same level.

Instinctively, Liane parted her legs, hooking them around his waist and dragging him in close, putting them chest to chest. Instantly she knew it wasn’t enough, that she needed skin to skin, and pulled back again, scrabbling to unfasten her jacket and drag it off. She couldn’t get the buttons of her shirt undone; one of them popped off and she started to laugh.

“Help!”

“I got you.” His hands were warm and steady as he took over, slipping the buttons free and pushing the shirt back off her shoulders.

“I wish I’d worn nicer underwear,” Liane mourned with a glance down at her plain black cotton bra.

“It’s what’s inside it that counts.” His grin was wicked as his hand slipped behind her back to deftly unfasten the clasp.

"Not much of that, either!"

"More than a handful's a waste, I reckon." The bra was flung aside, and then he was filling his hands, leaning in to kiss her again.

He was rock-hard, a heavy bar pushing at her through layers of clothes. She couldn't get enough, enough friction, enough of his taste. She raked blunt nails down his back, jerked her mouth free of his. "Bedroom. Actually, bathroom first. Condoms in the cabinet."

"Point me in the right direction." He gathered her up, taking her weight easily.

She still tightened her legs around his waist, a little nervous of being dropped. "Back through that door, then the next door down the hall."

"I got you." He didn't seem to be having any trouble at all with her, even freeing one hand to turn the handle on her bedroom door, before laying her down on the bed. "And… bathroom?"

"In there. They're in the cabinet over the sink."

He was back in a moment, dropping the box on the nightstand next to the book she was reading, glancing at it with a grin. “Andy Weir? Somehow I didn’t quite peg you for a science fiction reader.”

“He tells a good yarn. Shut up about my reading taste and get those jeans off.” She hadn’t been idle while he was gone, stripping off her boots and socks, now working on her belt.

“Yes, ma’am.”

“And definitely don’t call me that! We’re not in the military and you’re not under orders!” She was laughing, though, and so was he as he unfastened his belt.

“What, don’t you want to give me orders?” He was playful, and she was utterly charmed.

And, she had to admit, extremely turned on. They were both naked now, and Drew set a knee on the bed and crawled in over her, kissing her long and slow before he eased back down the bed to devote his attention to her breasts, kissing and licking and suckling on her nipples until her eyes rolled back in her head, soft, desperate moans spilling from her lips.

Liane's hard attitude disappeared in bed, Drew thought as he caressed her, admiring her body, lean and strong. The body of a woman who worked hard, and she had the hands to match, with short ragged nails, scrapes and nicks here and there, toughened skin on her palms. Her breasts were small, but beautifully shaped, her nipples plump and juicy, tight peaks in his mouth. He grinned with amusement as he slid lower and found a tuft of blonde which definitely didn't match the black and purple hair on her head.

"A natural blonde?"

"Sh, don't tell anyone. It's a secret."

They both started laughing again.

He liked her so damn much. Liked her no-nonsense attitude and quick wit, her dry humor and willingness to laugh at herself. Letting go was going to be hell, he already knew, but she'd made it clear that a few physical encounters was all she could offer, and he considered himself lucky to get that much.

Right now, he was determined to make sure she was having a damn good time, so he carried on shuffling down the bed until he was lying between her thighs, her legs over his shoulder, face buried in her groin, tongue working slow and gentle to lave her delicate bud. At least, he was trying to be slow and gentle, but that didn't last long as Liane tightened her legs around his neck, grabbed a handful of his hair and urged;

"More!"

He gave it to her, adding a finger, sliding up inside her channel, finding it already slick and oh so hot. A second finger and she moaned, hips coming up off the bed, rolling into the thrust of his fingers. He edged his thumb up between the soft petals of her labia, flicking at the underside of her clit even as his tongue worked over the top.

"Oh fuck. Yes. Yes, don't you dare stop, ah, there, right there!"

It wasn't long at all before Liane was very nearly screaming her demands, and he sure wasn't going to let her down. He kept working, tongue dancing, fingers pumping, until he felt the telltale flutter and clench in her walls, and then he slowed, not stopping completely, just stroking her through it, prolonging the orgasm for her.

"Day-um," Liane whispered raggedly a couple of minutes later.

"You okay?" He eased back, smirking a little, but it was hard not to feel smug when she'd just come hard on his fingers and tongue.

"Phew." She stared up at the ceiling, breathing fast, her fingers still gripping his hair tight. "I will be in a minute. Come up here." Her fingers unclenched, her hand falling away to pat the bed beside her. "A cuddle would be nice."

"Cuddle sounds fantastic." He honestly couldn't recall the last time he'd cuddled with anyone. Settling on his side beside her, he curved an arm lightly over her waist, tightening it as she rolling to face him, aligning their bodies, and pressed her face against his neck.

He could feel her pulse still hammering, her skin heated, sheened lightly with sweat. One hand skimmed over his hip, worked in between them.

“No hurry,” he said, but the words cut off in a strangled groan as she wrapped her hand tightly around his cock and squeezed.

He was already hard. Her strong, confident clasp brought him right up almost to the point of explosion. “Okay, now I am in a hurry.”

Her laugh was throaty and confident. “Grab those condoms, soldier. I have to get back to work in a bit.”

Drew would have preferred to stay here in bed with her for the whole day, making love and exploring their connection slow and leisurely, but he obeyed, reaching out a slightly shaking hand.

Liane took the condom from him and rolled it on expertly, before pushing him to his back and straddling his hips. He was very far from objecting, admiring her as she rose up and positioned herself over him, easing the tip of his cock inside her before stilling.

"Holy shit," Drew muttered, his throat dry. He drank her in with his eyes, this beautiful, confident, strong woman who had no hesitation in saying what she wanted and going after it.

She was sexy as hell, and it took every bit of willpower he had to hold still and let her take him at her own pace, not to shove up and thrust deep inside her. He'd got her nice and slick, but he wasn't small, and he didn't want to hurt her.

"Hell," Liane muttered as she sank down, slow and easy. Her thighs quivered as Drew put his hands on them, and he realized she wasn't quite as casual as she seemed.

"Easy," he whispered.

"So full," she panted back, half-laughing.

"It's okay, take your time."

"But I don't want to! Feels so good." She wiggled, slid down the last inch. Their groins met.

Drew couldn't contain the groan which burst from him, or the desperate need to move. He jack-knifed upwards, stomach muscles clenching, rather than buck his hips up. Desperately, he sought with his mouth, catching one of Liane's swollen nipples and sucking hard, urging with his hands on her thighs as she began to rock against him.

"Yes." She grasped his shoulders, bracing herself on him, and rode him like a damn mustang, accelerating the rocking rhythm of her hips.

He wasn't going to last long, but thankfully it seemed Liane was making sure she had a good time as well, because just as he felt the fireworks begin to explode up his spine, she stilled and gasped, bowing forward, holding them tight together.

"Faaaark!" Drew almost screamed it as the climax ripped out of him. He clung to Liane, not entirely sure where he ended and she began as they shuddered together.

She collapsed against him, suddenly limp, and he fell back against the pillow.

"I did not expect that to feel that good," Liane mumbled against his chest.

“That was…” He couldn’t even think of any words to describe it. Spectacular seemed to undersell it by quite a lot. In the end he settled for “Wow.”

She chuckled, and the delicate flutter of clenching internal muscles made his eyes roll back in his head again. “That about covers it, yeah.”

They lay entwined, still breathing hard, for several minutes. Drew would have happily stayed there for the rest of the day, but Liane finally sighed and eased back, slipping off him.

“I need to take a shower.”

“You want me to go?”

“No hurry.” She flapped a hand at him. “Stay there a bit. Wish I could stay there with you, but it’ll be getting busy downstairs in a bit.”

“I should get back over to Bull’s. He’s got me doing some maintenance on his van.”

Liane paused, halfway to the bathroom door. “Yeah? He doesn’t use that van much. Has he got plans?”

“Not that he’s shared with me yet, but he did say he has an errand for me to run in a couple of days.” Drew sat up, watching her. “Do you have a tracker or anything you want me to put on it?”

“I’ve got someone keeping tabs on your phone,” she said. “It’s a hella basic one they gave you, but it still has to ping cell towers. A tracker on the van would be too risky, I think. The Brethren might act crude but they’re more technologically sophisticated than you’d think. Cash has a degree in electrical engineering.”

“Damn,” Drew said, finding he wasn’t all that surprised. The club’s secretary was a quiet man, but there was always calculation going on behind his eyes, and Bull trusted him more than anyone, even his own nephew Kaleb. “Yeah. He might find a tracker.”

“Whatever errand it is, unless you are literally being sent to kill someone, just do it. I know it goes against the grain to run guns or drugs, but this will be a test. They’re not going to trust you with anything big until you’ve proved yourself on the small stuff. Whatever it is, report back to me afterwards and we’ll pass it on to my bosses to decide what to do about it."

"And if I am literally being sent to kill someone? They know I was a sniper. And I don't kid myself - sniper is just another word for government-sanctioned assassin. They don't have the Manhunters anymore to clean up their mess."

Liane made a face at the mention of the serial killer gang, sitting back down on the edge of the bed. "I think... play it exactly like that. Tell them that you quit being an assassin and you're not keen to get back into the game. Act stroppy. Ask if they're setting you up for a murder rap. Tell whoever gives you the order to do their own fucking dirty work. Undercover police work absolves a lot of sins, but murder's not one of them. Self-defense is another matter, of course."

"Have you?" he asked, curious.

"Killed in self-defense? Yes. Twice. I've also been in on several agency actions where things went south and the bullets started flying, and I shot criminals then, too." Her blue eyes were steady. "You don't have to worry about me being hesitant to pull the trigger, if it comes down to it."

"After seeing you at the range, I wasn't worried."

"We both know the range isn't real life."

He nodded in acknowledgment, and she nodded back before getting up again and heading into the bathroom. The shower started running and Drew lay back again, thinking over what she'd said. Running a few scenarios through his mind and planning what he might say if Bull did indeed give him an order he couldn't carry out.

Chapter Thirteen

Coming back from the bathroom, toweling her hair dry, Liane paused a moment to appreciate the naked man in her bed. Lying with his hands behind his back, gazing up at the ceiling, Drew was a sight to behold.

"You want anything to eat? I was going to make myself a quick sandwich before I go down."

"Sounds good," he agreed, looking across at her, before rolling upright to grab his clothes. Those that were in the bedroom, anyway. She grinned at the memory of of dragging his shirt off him in the kitchen.

Drew was watching her as she dressed, and Liane took her time about it, deliberately digging through her underwear drawer to find something a bit nicer than her usual plain black cotton. She couldn't find anything which matched... but she did find a white silk pair of boyleg panties and a pale blue lacy bra, and the expression on Drew's face as she put them on made the effort worth it.

"Put your tongue back in," she said teasingly, grabbing clean jeans from a drawer. "I don't have time."

"Uh huh."

He was still staring, and it was gratifying as hell. Liane came in for her fair share of male attention - not just the persistent Gerry, there were plenty of other guys in Redstone Creek who'd tried to get in her pants - but she almost always had the distinct impression they were more interested in her as a successful business owner than her as a woman.

The appreciation in Drew's eyes was all about her as a woman, and it made a curious, entirely unfamiliar warmth swell in her chest.

Deliberately, she turned her face away and finished dressing. You can't afford to let your emotions get involved here, she chided herself silently. This is just sex, you said so yourself. Blowing off steam, releasing tension with the one man in this town you can actually trust.

She still couldn't halt the damn butterflies in her stomach when he caught her elbow and drew her in to plant a lingering, heated kiss on her lips before letting go and heading off to the kitchen to find the rest of his clothes.

Liane puffed out a breath of air. Collapsed back against the wall before shaking her head. "Pull yourself together, girl," she muttered. "You're in the home stretch now. Don't get distracted."

One step at a time. Break down the tasks in front of her into smaller, manageable components. Compartmentalize. Stuff away the complicated, messy emotions she was in no place to deal with right now.

When are you ever in a place to deal with your emotions? a small voice in the back of her head asked, tone dry.

It sounded very much like the voice of her long-dead sister.

“Shut up, Kels,” Liane whispered back.

Stop living your life for me and start living it for you, Lee. Start living your life.

“I don’t even know what my life is,” she muttered under her breath. “I’m an undercover agent. That’s it.”

Yet as she left the bedroom and headed back to the kitchen, she caught a glimpse of Drew, sitting down at the table putting his boots on, and her heart gave a funny little jump.

Maybe it’s just my damn biological clock going off. Picking out a good stud to father my children. And where did THAT thought come from?

Liane shook her head, half-laughing at herself. Having children wasn’t a thought which had ever even crossed her mind until that moment.

“Care to let me in on the joke?” Drew asked curiously.

“Just a passing thought.” She opened the refrigerator, pulled out a package of turkey, some Swiss cheese and a bag of mixed salad. “Turkey sandwich?”

"Sounds good."

"Mustard, mayo or both?"

"Definitely both, please."

She added a pickle and a handful of potato chips to the side of each plate, and he thanked her as she set one down in front of him.

"Iced tea?" Liane offered. "Proper sweet tea. I make it myself," she added when he gave her a narrow-eyed look.

"Georgia girl," he murmured.

"Virginia, actually. My grandmother really is from Georgia, but my Southern habits are all Virginia. It's where I grew up - though my cover story says I'm from Detroit."

"Got family in Virginia still?"

"My mom. She and my father parted ways a few years ago. He's with the State Department, accepted a cushy posting to run the American consulate in Barcelona, Spain. Mom used to be a lobbyist, but she retired. She's not slowing down, though. She bought

into a yoga studio run by her long-time yoga instructor."

"Any siblings?"

"One sister. She's in Silicon Valley somewhere."

Drew gave her raised eyebrows. "Somewhere?"

"She's kind of secretive about it. She was with the NSA - she's a computer whizzkid. But she got recruited for some kind of private security group and moved to their headquarters in California."

"Sounds like a useful person to know. Especially with suspected leaks in one or other of the interested agencies on this case."

The comment hit Liane like a bolt of lightning. Of course. She'd been wary of passing on certain details to her boss, just in case her cover might get compromised. But Jessikah - Jessikah was someone Liane could trust absolutely, and she wasn't bound by agency protocols. Maybe she could figure out exactly where the leak was coming from. Help them plug it before someone else got hurt.

"I have to go," Drew said, rising to his feet. "Thanks for the sandwich."

She'd been eating mechanically, staring into space while she thought about how to contact Jessikah. She needed a new phone. A burner. But a smartphone, one she could use to send emails. Bad idea to buy one in Redstone Creek, where who knew might be watching, but every month or so she drove down to Coeur d'Alene to pick up supplies for the roadhouse which were difficult to get locally. She was about due a trip.

"See you soon." Drew bent to kiss her, and she reached up to touch his cheek.

"Be careful."

"Always. You too." He stroked his fingers through her hair, stealing another kiss before heading on out. Liane put their plates in the dishwasher, still thinking about how she was going to get in touch with her sister and exactly what she would ask Jessikah to do for her.

“Good, you’re back.” Bull walked out of the house as Drew pulled up in front of the garage.

“Figured I could get that oil change finished this evening.” Drew nodded deferentially.

“You do that, and then we have a job to do. Come knock on the door once you’re finished.”

What job? Drew wondered. And just him and Bull? That never happened. Kaleb was always around. He shrugged compliantly, though. “Yes, sir.”

“Ain’t kicked those military habits yet, eh?” Bull grinned and spat in the dirt. “Don’t mind bein’ called sir, really. More respect than some of the boys show.”

Drew didn’t say anything to that. He recognized the trap. Criticize any of the Brethren’s full members, and he’d be seen as a traitor. It wasn’t his place, not while he was still a prospect.

“I’ll get to work. Anything else you need?”

"You can clean out the driver's cabin. Don't touch the outside, though. Or anything in the back."

"Got it." Again, Drew didn't ask questions, and Bull nodded, a satisfied smile on his lips.

It wasn't much more than an hour later that Drew knocked on the internal door leading into the house and called "I'm done!"

"Coming," Bull called back, and came out a few minutes later, shrugging into his cut. "Get on your bike. We've got a job to do."

"We picking up Kaleb?"

"Not tonight."

Bull didn't say anything more, and a knot of nervous tension lodged in Drew's gut as he followed the Brethren's president through the darkening streets to Cash's house, where they found Cash and Gerry both waiting for them. Neither spoke, just fired up their bikes, and Bull pulled out again.

For a brief moment, Drew thought they were going to the roadhouse, but they pulled into the lot further up the street, the garage where the Brethren sometimes got major work on their bikes done.

"What's going on?" Drew asked as he followed the other three men, dismounting their bikes and walking around to the back of the building. A trailer was parked there, a light on inside. "Who's here?"

"Tom Salz." It was Cash who answered him.

"The bike mechanic?"

"Yeah." Gerry hawked and spat. "The new guy in town. The other new guy in town." He gave Drew a side-eye.

"Drew's vouched for, Gerry. He's family. Jacob's cousin." Bull gave Gerry a not-too-friendly push as the four of them approached the trailer. "Tom, though? A bike mechanic that good doesn't just turn up and settle in a nowhere town like Redstone Creek. Too much money in a big city for that. He shouldn't be here."

"I don't get it," Drew said, playing dumb, as Gerry hammered on the little trailer's door.

"He's a fucking plant. An undercover Fed. We know there's one in town. Got it confirmed yesterday. It's gotta be him. So we're gonna let him know we know, and then we're gonna give him the choice of getting out of town before dawn or leaving in a pine box."

The door swung open and the scent of marijuana smoke wafted out. Drew raised his eyebrows. Stared at Bull.

"Sure don't smell like a fed," he drawled sarcastically. "You sure you got the right man?"

"Nope," Gerry growled, glaring at Drew, but Bull cuffed him upside the head.

"Yes. Get out here, Salz!"

"Bull?" The mechanic, a thin, bearded guy with long hair in a ratty ponytail and the hazy expression of someone who'd just done a fair amount of weed, stood framed in the doorway, blinking slowly at them. "What's up, man?"

"Get him." Bull nudged Drew. "We're gonna take him inside."

Cash was already unlocking the rear door to the mechanic's shop. Drew spared only a moment to wonder where he'd got the keys before he moved into action, stepping forward to grab Salz's ponytail and haul him out of the trailer.

"Hey!" Salz wailed, tried to push him off, but Drew had probably sixty pounds on him in solid muscle, six inches of height and a whole lot of Special Forces training and fighting experience. Salz didn't stand a chance.

Cash lashed a rope around Salz's hands; Gerry pulled a hook on a chain down from the ceiling and they hung the protesting mechanic, rapidly coming down from his high, up so that his toes just barely brushed the floor.

"Work him over." Bull pointed at Drew. "I want confirmation of what agency he's with."

Drew could only hope the mechanic really was an agent, because otherwise he was about to get beaten up for nothing. At least Bull seemed inclined to let him leave town alive. He told himself that as he stepped forward and plowed a fist into Salz's gut.

Half an hour later, Salz had spilled his entire sorry life story, none of which involved being a federal agent. Quite the opposite. He was in hiding after getting caught up in a high-end ring of thieves, who'd been stealing premium cars and motorbikes and shipping them out of the country. Salz had fled clear across the country from New Jersey, taking the job in Redstone Creek in a desperate effort to stay off the radar of the authorities looking for him.

"He's not a fed," Cash said in disgust at last, staring at the sobbing man hanging limply from the chain. "Just a dickhead."

"What do you want to do, boss?" Drew affected casualness, shaking out his fists. He'd made it look worse than it was, not that Salz knew that. Drew had pulled punches that could have pulverized organs and bone, instead leaving just bruises. The worst he'd done was knock out a couple of teeth.

"Let him go," Bull said finally. "Same plan." He stepped up to stare into Salz's face. "You got until sunrise to git gone. And if I ever see your face in my town again, I'll let him finish the job." He nodded at Drew.

“I’m gone,” Salz snivelled. “I promise. You’ll never see me again. I don’t know what I did to piss you off, but I promise, I ain’t no fed!”

“Yeah. I believe you.” Bull sounded thoroughly pissed off. “Let him down, Cash. Drew. Clean him up, help him pack his shit, escort him out of town. Before sunrise.”

“Yes, sir.”

“Bull,” Gerry said, his tone nearly a whine, “you’re forgetting something. We know there’s an agent. If it ain’t Salz…”

“Fucking drop it, Gerry!” Bull turned on him in a rage. “We know it ain’t Drew, either! There’s plenty of other folks in this town it could be.”

Gerry retreated, grumbling, casting poisonous glances in Drew’s direction. Drew ignored him, helping Cash let Salz down and hauling Salz upright when he collapsed, dragging the man’s arm over his shoulder.

“Come on, buddy. We gotta get you out of town.”

“Y’all just beat me up, I ain’t gonna let you help me!”

Drew sighed. “I was just following orders, man. C’mon. Let me help you pack, or you’ll be leaving behind more than you want to. You should probably take some Tylenol, too.”

Salz grumbled, but he didn’t try to pull away, letting Drew help him back to his seedy, weed-scented trailer.

It was going to be a long damn night, Drew thought as Salz asked him to pull his truck around so he could start loading his belongings into the back. He allowed himself a few moments to think wistfully of Liane, of how incredible she’d felt in his arms that afternoon, before sighing and getting to work.

Chapter Fourteen

"Hey."

Busy stacking glasses as she unloaded the dishwasher, Liane hadn't heard Drew come in. She jumped and shot him a filthy look. He offered an apologetic smile.

"Sorry. Didn't mean to startle you."

"At least I didn't break any glasses," she grumbled, but it was hard to stay grumpy when he was leaning on the bar looking so handsome. She walked out from behind the bar and reached up to hook her arms around his neck, draw him around for a kiss. "So what brings you around here before the bar opens?" She saw him most days, though he was never able to stay overnight. Just over a week since they'd first slept together, they'd had little opportunity since, and Liane was definitely starting to feel like she had an itch that needed scratching.

"Just wanted to let you know I'm not gonna be around for a couple of days. Going on an errand."

"Oh?" Something about the way he said it set off warning bells in Liane's mind, and she stopped thinking about her libido for a minute. "Somewhere special?"

"Not exactly sure, to be honest. Over the border somewhere. I'll get details when I get closer, but I've been told to head for Edmonton."

"On your bike?"

"Nah. Taking Bull's van."

It was a smuggling run, Liane instantly realized. Though whether Drew was taking something into Canada or bringing something else back - or possibly even both - she didn't know. And quite possibly, neither did he.

"You going on your own?"

"No, Kaleb's coming with."

They were alone in the bar at that moment, but Liane still barely breathed the words as she leaned in, her lips close to Drew's ear. "It's a test."

"Of course," he murmured back, nuzzling her neck. "Not the first. Bull's showed me a hidden compartment under the van's floor, but it's not big enough."

She understood what he meant. Whatever could fit into that compartment wasn't enough to make this the major route the Brethren used to smuggle whatever it was they were moving. Bull's van rarely left his garage, besides.

"Okay. Well, I guess I'll see you when you get back." Nobody was watching, so she didn't have to do it, but she still pulled his face down to hers and kissed him, long and slow. "Be careful," she whispered against his lips.

"Always." He lifted his head, smiled down at her. "I've been practicing with my new pistol."

"You're taking it with you?"

"Secret compartment," he reminded her.

"Fair point." She felt a little better knowing he'd be armed. And that Kaleb was with him, because she was pretty sure that Bull was actually very fond of Kaleb and wouldn't knowingly put his nephew in harm's way. "Well. Have a good trip. Bring me back some maple syrup."

He laughed, as she'd meant him to. "I'll text you when I'm on my way back."

That would be a normal thing to do and shouldn't arouse any suspicion. She nodded, accepting it, kissed him once more and watched him leave. Calling to her staff that she was just going up to her apartment for a few minutes, she rushed upstairs, took her recently-purchased burner phone out of the secret compartment she'd built for it inside a fake shampoo bottle, and typed a message to Jessikah.

Drew's on the move. Can you track?

Not as accurately as if he had a GPS phone, but yes, her sister replied only a couple of minutes later.

Liane grimaced, wishing the Brethren weren't quite so paranoid. None of them had smartphones, only basic flip phones, obviously worried about being tracked. Which she absolutely would have done, of course. But the tech department at ATF insisted the flip phones weren't trackable.

Jessikah disagreed. She might not be able to pinpoint the phone to a single square meter, but she could certainly triangulate well enough to get a street address. Or so she claimed.

Map where and when and let me have it please, Liane texted back.

You got it.

Jessikah hadn't seemed in the least surprised when Liane reached out, and Liane was pretty sure her sister was already keeping tabs on her. She wasn't entirely sure how to feel about that - Jessikah was her younger sister, after all.

Putting the phone away again, Liane made her way slowly back downstairs. She had the sensation that things were accelerating, coming to a head.

She just hoped she'd be there when the fuze finally blew, and Drew wouldn't be left standing alone in the eye of the storm.

"Next left," Kaleb said abruptly, and Drew nodded, putting the blinker on. The van was nondescript-looking but smooth handling, and he suspected it had been through more than one unobtrusive upgrade since it left the factory.

"We nearly there? My butt is numb," he grumbled.

"Another mile."

They were driving through an industrial zone on the outskirts of Edmonton. It was Saturday evening, most of the businesses were shut down for the weekend, and there were few other vehicles on the road.

"That gate right there," Kaleb said finally.

"Place looks abandoned," Drew muttered darkly.

"What, you want them to put on a light show to welcome us? Drive around the back. You'll see an open door: drive right in."

Kaleb had seemed to get more confident as they drove. Weirdly eager, in fact. Like he was looking forward to some kind of treat. He'd refused to talk about what they were transporting - it had apparently already been loaded before Drew got to Bull's house that morning - or what they'd be picking up, or anything about the people they were coming to meet.

Driving in through the door, Drew turned his headlights on, because the interior of the warehouse was black as pitch, and it only got darker as the door rattled down behind them.

"Stop here, and turn the damn lights off!" Kaleb instructed.

"What, do you have night vision I don't know about?" but Drew obeyed. As soon as the van's engine died, some lights clicked on; low and localized, they wouldn't be visible outside to anyone who might be passing by. He made out three figures standing in front of the van.

"Out slowly," Kaleb said. "Keep your hands showing."

"This the new guy, Kaleb?" a voice called as they got out of the van. "Bull said he's Jacob's cousin?"

"That's right, this is Drew. Our new brother," Kaleb answered, and as the speaker moved forward, Drew had to work not to gasp with shock, because the man was wearing a Brethren vest.

I didn't know there was a chapter in Canada. Does Liane know, I wonder?

"This is Valdosta," Kaleb introduced. "The local vice-president. He reports to Bull."

Interesting - the chapter doesn't have their own president - so it's more of a sub-chapter. Bull's not good at giving up control.

Drew shook hands with Valdosta, offering a respectful nod. The other two men were moving forward, going to open the van's sliding door and unloading the boxes inside - full of innocuous cheap goods - before accessing the hidden compartment beneath the floor.

Valdosta didn't even bother to watch, which confirmed Drew's suspicions that this run wasn't carrying anything of any real significance. He watched from the corner of his eye as the unloading continued. Guns, he realized, which made sense. They were definitely easier to get ahold of in Idaho than here in Canada. Half a dozen compact automatic rifles, with high-capacity magazines. He'd let Liane know, and no doubt ATF would pass the information on to their Canadian counterparts, but it was small potatoes compared to what they knew the Brethren had been moving around.

Some different boxes were being brought forward on a wheeled trolley, and Drew watched unobtrusively as flat boxes stamped with the logo of a major pharmaceutical company were loaded into the hidden compartment before it was closed and cartons full of maple syrup were put into the van's main bay.

"That's it, then?" he asked as the van door slid closed. "Are we off again?"

"Not just yet." Kaleb grinned, an anticipatory, feral smirk. "We have some merchandise to inspect."

Valdosta grinned too. "Your favorite part, Kaleb. We have an excellent selection this time. We'll take them to the halfway house tonight and be ready to move them through to you on the fourth. Come on in."

Them? Sudden foreboding swept through Drew. He followed close behind Kaleb as Valdosta led them through the warehouse to a locked door, pulling a key from around a chain on his neck to open the padlock.

"I'm the only one with a key to this door," Valdosta noted, catching Drew looking at the key as he tucked it back inside his shirt. "Avoids interference with the merchandise."

The smell hit him first. The smell of unwashed bodies… and the stench of terror.

Behind the door was hell.

A row of cages, down each side of a room at least twenty meters in length, each cage holding two or three cowering women or… Drew had to swallow bile. There were children in some of the cages. A boy no older than six or seven stared at him from wide, terrified eyes, even as an older girl tried to shove him behind her.

"You've got a good assortment," Kaleb noted, his tone so casual he might have been discussing the weather as he walked down the aisle between the cages. "Not all Mexican this time."

"Bull told us he needed a variety. We found a decent source bringing in Chinese families, and we've got a couple of good recruiters operating in different cities looking for Caucasian girls. Good prices on young white girls, and if they're already whining about running away from home, the police don't bother looking too hard."

Drew bit on the inside of his cheek until he tasted blood, using the pain to keep him focused. Catalog what you see. Find out what you can about how these people are going to be smuggled over the border. Don't let the Brethren know how much this sickens you.

"See anything you like, Kaleb?" Valdosta said, his voice teasing.

"Oh, a few." Kaleb laughed, his expression avid as he moved closer to one cage. "This one. What's your name, sweetheart?"

It was the girl who'd tried to shield the little boy. Drew didn't think she could be any more than twelve years old, a pretty, delicate Chinese girl. She stared at Kaleb from wide, defiant dark eyes but didn't speak.

"No English," Valdosta said with a shrug.

"She won't need it." Kaleb laughed crudely. He pulled something from his pocket and lifted it; a camera, Drew realized as the flash went off.

"I'll show her to Bull, but I think she's probably the one. That said, you've got a nice selection. We might even keep two."

I don't know Kaleb at all. It was a shock to the system for Drew, and he realized he'd been lulled by Kaleb's youth and affability. This, in front of him, this was the real Kaleb, practically slavering over a girl so young she hadn't even hit puberty.

No wonder Kaleb's not bothered about his supposed girlfriend at the high school. She's too old for his tastes.

Kaleb was walking down the aisle between the cages, taking photographs of the occupants of each. Drew made himself follow, even while a part of his mind was calculating the odds of taking down Kaleb, Valdosta and the other two men right here and now and summoning the authorities to free the prisoners. He could do it, he thought, even without his gun, which contrary to what he'd told Liane, he'd had to leave behind. The problem was that he couldn't be sure if any other members of the local Brethren chapter were in the building, and they were in a remote and isolated enough spot that very likely even shots being fired wouldn't bring the authorities around to investigate.

Glancing around, Drew discovered he was being watched; the two men who'd unloaded the van were watching from the door, both of them with hands resting casually inside their jackets. So they didn't trust him entirely, were watching to see if he reacted badly to the sight of the prisoners. He breathed slowly, ordered his face to remain neutral, and followed Kaleb.

Deal with it later. Liane will help.

The problem was, he wasn't sure if Liane's bosses would. Human trafficking wasn't within ATF's purview, and with a mole inside either the DEA or FBI - possibly both - passing the information along might be signing both his and Liane's death warrants as well as those of the prisoners.

The only thing Drew was sure of was that he would not allow these women and children to be trafficked into the US and sold on to God only knew where, with one or more unfortunates to be kept to be the Brethren's playthings... for however long they lasted. He could not. So he followed and listened, expression blank, hoping for some crumbs of information about how and when the prisoners were to be moved over the border.

This was where it ended. He didn't care which law enforcement agency got the credit. He'd make sure Liane got out safe. But there was no way he was letting Kaleb get his hands on that little Chinese girl, or any of the others.

No. Fucking. Way.

Chapter Fifteen

"Human trafficking?" Liane looked as sick as Drew still felt, even a full day after seeing that warehouse in Edmonton and the terrified occupants of those cages.

"Women and children," Drew confirmed. "No men at all. I probed as much as I dared and Kaleb basically said that men are too much trouble, even if you sell them as slave labor. They prefer women under the age of twenty-five, they'll take girls at any age and boys up to the age of thirteen or so. Pretty much all destined for the sex trade."

"How many?" She sank heavily into a chair at her kitchen table, her face anguished.

"There were seventeen in the cages, and Valdosta said they expected a couple more in the next few days before the transfer on the fourth."

"The fourth of July?"

"Must be. Again, I didn't want to press too much, but I can't imagine they'd want to keep them another month. They'd have to feed them. The fourth is less than a week away."

"I still don't understand how they're getting them across the border, and what they're doing with them once they're here. I never had a clue they were moving people in these sorts of numbers!"

"I can't let it happen." He didn't know how to explain himself. "I can't, Liane. I know your bosses probably don't have what they need to prosecute. I'm sorry. I just can't let Kaleb get his hands on that little girl. The way he looked at her, I..."

"Drew." She reached out, put her hand over his fist, clenched on the table in front of him. "I'm with you. There are some things that can't be tolerated. Everyone has their lines in the sand. If I'd been in your place in that warehouse, we'd be sitting here now having this exact same conversation. This is where it stops."

"Thank you." He made himself take a deep breath. "I wanted to stop it right then and there. Take down Kaleb and Valdosta and the other two and bust all those cages open."

Liane's eyes were soft as she watched him, nodding slowly. "We're going to stop it, I promise. You did well to hold yourself back."

"It nearly broke me," he admitted. "I still want to just lose it and beat Kaleb to a pulp. I hate the fact that I'd kind of liked him, up until that moment."

"To be completely honest, I kind of did too. That's the problem with pedophiles, though - they don't go around with a big flashing signal over their heads so we can recognize them. They don't let you know who they really are unless and until they believe you're one of them."

"Which means I've been pretty damn convincing at making the Brethren think I'm as sick as they are." The feeling wrenched at Drew's guts.

"Which means you've done a good job on your first undercover assignment," Liane corrected him.

"Doesn't really feel like it. I let the guns go through into Canada and that was a decent load of opiates we brought back." He shook his head. "I don't like just letting things happen. My military career was all about taking decisive - often preventative - action."

"Sure, but there must have been a lot of times when you just had to wait for the right target to be in just the right place at exactly the right moment," Liane pointed out. "And that's what's happened now. We catch the Brethren in the act with these trafficking victims, they're going down."

"But we can't do it without more manpower, and your bosses..."

Liane raised a brow and smiled coolly. "My bosses? All they're going to know is that you have intel that a large load of merchandise is being brought over the border on the fourth. What exactly is in that shipment isn't clear at this moment, but... we're talking several hundred kilos of product. I'll tell them once they're committed to action, exactly what the merchandise is."

Product. Merchandise. Just referring to the women and children he'd seen in those terms made Drew's stomach churn even harder, but Liane was right. ATF would only help if they thought the shipment might be their problem, and they couldn't risk passing the intel to the FBI or DEA. If the mole passed the information back to the Brethren, the trafficked women and children would vanish and Drew would be directly in the Brethren's sights as the person who must have turned on them.

It occurred to him suddenly that there was another interested party, and someone he could absolutely trust. The man who'd sent him here in the first place.

"Jason Hunter," he said out loud. "He's going to want to know, and I'm one hundred per cent sure we can trust him."

Liane hummed under her breath, sat back in her chair and scrunched her face up, obviously thinking. "I guess you're obliged to report to him?" she said, her tone questioning. Obviously giving Drew the opening to say yes, he absolutely was required to report to Jason. Leaving the choice up to him.

“Yes,” he said, not at all truthfully, and saw from her quirky smile that she was well aware he was lying to her.

“Then you need to do that soon. I bought a spare burner phone the other day, if you want to use it to contact him. Just don’t let yourself be caught with it.” She got up and crouched down in front of the stove, carefully removed the base panel and reached up underneath. A moment later she put a phone down on the table in front of him, a smartphone, he saw with some relief.

“It’s charged and there’s plenty of credit on it. There’s a number saved under ‘Sis’.” She hesitated a moment, but then carried on. “My sister Jessikah’s number. She’ll help you out if you can’t get hold of me.”

“The hacker?” he queried.

“Yeah. I reached out to her for some off-the-books work. I want to try and figure out who the Brethren’s mole is, and my bosses don't seem inclined to go digging in other agencies' business in case they step on toes." She made a face, clearly showing what she thought of inter-agency politics. "Jess is going to tug on some threads. See if she can find anything."

"She knows about me?" he checked, pocketing the phone after checking the ringtone was on silent.

"Yeah, I told her. And just to illustrate that she can get into any database she damn well pleases, she had your unredacted military service record up on her screen in under five minutes."

Drew nodded, suitably impressed. Getting those wouldn't be simple unless you were at a pretty high level in the Rangers, or even higher in the Pentagon. That a civilian was able to do it was impressive... if slightly worrying.

"She did note that she thought you were kinda hot," Liane added with a grin.

"Only kinda hot?" He smiled too, feeling a little of his tension drain away as she lightened the tone of the conversation. Standing up, he reached for her hand, drew her up to stand with him.

“In her defense, the picture in your service record isn’t that flattering. You were a lot younger, too. You’re definitely glowing up.”

Drew had to laugh. God, he liked Liane so much. Liked her sense of humor, her unerring instinct for justice. He hadn’t known her all that long but he’d been utterly certain she’d back him against her bosses to save the trafficking victims - even though it might cost her career if her bosses found out she’d withheld information from them and potentially jeopardized the investigation.

“When we get out of this,” he said, ”if we get out of this...”

“Sshh.” She reached up, pressed the tip of her finger gently against his lips. “Don’t, Drew. It’s bad luck. Let’s just be grateful for the stolen moments we can have now.”

He wanted to argue. Wanted to tell her that he wasn’t prepared to just walk away, that when this mission was all over, he wanted a relationship with her, a real one. But he respected her wishes, nodded, and kissed her instead.

After the horrors Drew had just revealed to her, Liane wanted nothing more than to lose herself in him for a few hours. Soon enough she was going to have to contact her boss and pass on a judiciously edited report, in urgent enough terms that backup would be in place and ready to go on the fourth, because Drew was absolutely right. There was no way they could allow those women and children to be smuggled in and passed on to wherever they were destined to end up, and certainly the Brethren could not be allowed to keep and abuse the little girl Kaleb had selected. She was pretty sure her boss would agree with them, but unfortunately he'd also be obligated to pass the information on to the FBI, and if the mole was in the FBI, they'd be signing Drew's death warrant.

She pushed away her worries, letting herself sink into Drew's embrace. It was late; he'd arrived at the roadhouse just minutes before closing, helped her clean up and close the place down before accompanying her upstairs and making his report. She wasn't tired, though. Pulling back, she smiled up at Drew and tugged on his hand, drawing him along behind her as she headed for the bedroom.

"Can you stay tonight?" she asked as she peeled off her shirt.

"Yeah." He shrugged out of his cut, almost threw it across the room with barely concealed distaste, and shuddered. "God. I hate wearing that. Knowing now what they stand for... what they've done..."

"Hush." She shook her head at him. "It's just a costume, Drew. Just a role you're playing, like a Hollywood actor hired to play a villain. The role doesn't define who you are." She'd done months of training where those concepts were hammered into her, before she ever took on an undercover assignment, and watching Drew agonize now reminded her that he'd never had any of that training. That his qualification for this particular job was literally who he was related to and that he'd never have been placed undercover with the Brethren if his cousin hadn't been one of the gang.

Drew pulled his shirt off, lean muscles rippling in his torso, and Liane paused in her own undressing to stare appreciatively. "Damn, you are one fine looking man," she murmured.

"You know you said that out loud, right?" Drew cracked a small smile.

She grinned unrepentantly. "Hey, I'm literally talking to the one person I can be myself with. If I can't say whatever I'm thinking with you, when can I?"

"Good point." He sat down on the edge of the bed to pull his boots off, before reaching for her to pull her down onto his lap and kiss her, slow and lingering.

"You are the only good thing that's happened to me in longer than I can remember," she whispered against his lips, and he pulled back, looked in her eyes. At this close range, she could see the greyish clouding in his right eye, the way it didn't quite focus the same as his left, the pupil slow to react. See the fading pinkish lines of the scars beneath it, mute souvenirs to what he'd suffered.

"I feel the same way." He cupped her cheek lightly. "I'm so damn glad you're here, Liane. So glad."

Their lovemaking this time was slow. Almost leisurely, as they explored each others' bodies, kissing and tasting, touching, discovering the exact places and pressures which elicited gasps and moans. Whispering praises and pleas for more. And when Drew rose over Liane and slid slowly, easily into her eager, welcoming body, she hissed his name between her teeth and clawed at his shoulders, already so close to tipping over the edge. Wrapping her legs around his hips, she urged him on, demanding more, harder, now.

Drew groaned, throwing his head back, the cords in his neck standing out as he clenched his teeth. "Damn, woman. I'm too close. Easy…"

"No, please, I need it, now!" She almost sobbed, bucking against him. He felt so good inside her, hot and thick. And he knew exactly what she liked, putting pressure in all the right spots as he thrust, finding a rhythm that had her practically screaming the roof down.

“It’s a good thing you don’t have neighbors,” he mumbled against her throat a few minutes later, sounding as punch-drunk as she felt. “They’d be calling the cops on us for excessive noise.”

Liane started to giggle, putting still-shaking arms around his back and hugging tight. She didn’t want to let go, and Drew seemed to feel the same way, holding on to her in return. At length he eased back, rolling off and lying down beside her, but he immediately put an arm back over her again.

“Do you mind?” he murmured quietly. “It’s just been a really long time…”

“Without being held? Yeah. Me too.” Rolling to her side facing away from him, she wiggled backwards until she was curled tight against him. “You make a nice big spoon,” she mumbled, on the verge of sleep.

“Happy to be your big spoon anytime, beautiful.” He pressed warm lips to the back of her neck, the delicious heat of his body enveloping her, making her feel protected, safe, for the first time in months.

It was an illusion, of course. They were very far from safe. But just for tonight, Liane let herself pretend as she closed her eyes and drifted off to sleep.

Chapter Sixteen

Waking up in Drew Murphy's arms was a delightful experience, or it would have been, if five minutes later someone hadn't started banging on the door of Liane's apartment and yelling.

"What the fuck?" She scowled.

Drew groaned, falling to his back and putting his forearm across his eyes. "I dunno, but please, please get rid of them."

She grumbled under her breath as she got out of bed and yanked on a pair of yoga pants and Drew's T-shirt, the closest clothes to hand which would make her decent.

"I'm coming, keep your damn hair on!" she yelled as she strode barefoot across the apartment and yanked the door open, to come face to face with Bull, Kaleb lurking behind him. “What d'you want?” She glared at Bull.

“Is Drew here?”

“Sure, which you'd know if you'd bothered to call him. Or did you lose your phone?” She didn't step back to let him through the door, even though he moved forward as though he expected her to get out of the way. “Because I know Drew didn't switch his off. He's paranoid about it. Wants to make sure he can check how high if y'all want to tell him to jump.”

Kaleb barked out a laugh, but Bull's expression didn't change. “You going to keep us standing on the doorstep?”

She was tempted to say yes, but deliberately antagonizing him might make Drew's life more difficult. Instead she sighed exaggeratedly and stepped back, opening the door wider. “Fine. You better not have mud on your boots. I cleaned yesterday.”

They followed her to the living room, where she stood with arms folded and looked at them. Bull took a seat on her couch, looking quite comfortable in a room he'd never been in before, while Kaleb prowled over to the window, twitched the blinds aside and peered out.

"I'm gonna need my shirt back," Drew murmured behind her, and she turned to see he'd put on his jeans and boots. His cut dangled from one hand. With the other, he plucked lightly at the hem of the shirt she was wearing. "Any chance you could put one of your own on and give me this one back?"

She made a grumpy noise, but nodded. "Don't you dare put your feet on my coffee table," she said to Bull, who snorted. "I mean it. I'll put up with a lot but I swear, you put your feet on my table, you'll never eat another meal in my roadhouse that don't have spit in it."

Kaleb laughed again, and this time Bull cracked a smile too. He gave her a small nod.

"You're pushing your luck, woman." Drew patted her ass. "Get me that shirt back, or I'll take it off you right here and I don't care if they see your tits."

She flipped him the bird, plus a grin Kaleb and Bull wouldn't be able to see, as she flounced out and headed to the bedroom.

Drew leaned in the doorway and watched Bull and Kaleb. "What's the problem?" he drawled. Pulling his phone from his back pocket, he waggled it. "I've got no texts or missed calls. So what gives, that you just had to come here and annoy Liane?"

"This is news that has to be delivered in person." Bull got up off the couch, crossed the room and held his hand out to Drew. "Congratulations. We held a vote last night; you're now a full member of the Pure Brethren."

Drew's jaw dropped; he hadn't expected that. "What?"

"That run you went on up to Canada was a test. All the product went through at both ends with no trouble, no tracking devices found on them... and it was confirmed that the feds didn't have any whisper of our shipment coming in here."

Drew blinked, shaking Bull's offered hand. "Of course not. Wait." He feigned outrage. "Did you really think I was a fucking plant?"

"Not me," Bull shook his head.

"Fucking Gerry!" He didn't have to fake his distaste. "What the hell is his problem?"

"Let it go." Bull made a placating gesture.

"Did he vote for me to get full brotherhood?" Drew narrowed his eyes.

"He abstained," Kaleb put in, and Bull threw him an irritated look. Obviously, that was information Bull would have preferred Drew didn't have.

"It doesn't matter now. You're in." Bull clapped Drew on his still-bare shoulder. "And we've got work to do before our big shipment arrives on the fourth. So get your shirt on and let's get moving."

"Hmph." Drew pretended to accept Bull's word for it, turned as if to call for Liane, and spun back around. "Wait. What do you mean, confirmation that the feds didn't know about our shipment?"

"If you'd been a plant, you'd have passed on the information about what we brought back," Kaleb said. "You'd have been obliged to. And because of what it was, the DEA would have the information... and they don't."

"How do you know? Fuck." He let his eyes widen. "You have a source in the DEA?"

Footsteps presaged Liane's return, and both Bull and Kaleb clearly weren't going to say anything more with her there. She handed Drew his shirt, looking around curiously at the sudden dead silence which had fallen in the room.

"Well, since y'all are here, I guess I could make coffee. And breakfast... I could fix pancakes," she offered.

Kaleb, as always a bottomless pit when it came to food, agreed eagerly, and Bull surprised Drew by nodding.

"That'd be good, Liane. I'm hungry."

Liane looked surprised too, but she shrugged and went into the kitchen. "Kaleb, could you come and crack these eggs for me while I start the coffee?" Her voice floated back to them, and Kaleb went into the kitchen after her.

Drew looked back towards Bull just in time to see Bull slide his hand back from under the coffee table. It was an odd gesture, an awkward position for his hand to be in, and Drew's instincts were instantly on alert.

Did he just put something under there? A bug, maybe?

Pretending he hadn't seen anything, he shrugged on his shirt and then his cut, before flopping down into a chair and sighing exaggeratedly. "I was looking forward to another hour in bed, Bull. Way to kill the mood. Not that I'm not pleased to be elevated to full member, obviously!"

"You'll have plenty of time for fun later."

"Yeah. About that." Drew cast a pretend furtive glance towards the kitchen door, lowered his voice. "Liane don't care about guns or drugs as long as she don't see none of it here. But the, ah, the other merchandise Kaleb showed me? Don't think she'd like that too much. She wouldn't care about the foreigners, but there were white girls in the bunch." That should strike a nice balance, he thought, between making sure he played to Bull's racist prejudices and expressing some natural caution.

"She don't need to know about it." Bull shrugged. "They won't be here long. Got to get them to the auction."

"Auction?" Drew's ears pricked up, but he kept his expression dull.

"In Vegas, on the twelfth. They need to be there two days before so they can be examined and cataloged, so you can see we won't have much time. Whoever goes misses out on most of the fun time with what we keep for ourselves, though."

Drew had to fight down a shudder. "I guess that means I'll be going, as new boy. Long damn drive, to Vegas."

"Fraid so. We already drew lots for who'll go with you: Cash got the short straw."

"Could be worse. Could be Gerry."

Bull chuckled at Drew's deadpan remark. "Eh. Gerry's all right. He thinks you're after his job, since Jacob was sergeant-at-arms before him."

"I'd do it better than him, for sure." Drew shrugged. "But I'm still learning the ropes. I'll give him a year or two before I start really treading on his heels."

Bull seemed amused. "I like you, Drew, even if you are gonna cause trouble with Gerry. You got guts."

"Rangers didn't train me to be a pussy." And if he'd acted subservient, they might well have smelled a rat. He was walking a tightrope, trying to appear what they expected him to be all the time.

"Pancakes are ready!" Liane called from the kitchen then, and Drew almost sighed with relief, having got through yet another conversation with Bull without raising suspicions.

He hoped.

After breakfast, Bull and Kaleb told Drew he needed to go with them, and he nodded, getting up. He didn't apologize to Liane for leaving her to wash up, not verbally anyway.

"Walk us out, darlin'?" he said instead.

"Sure." She followed his lead without so much as a sideways glance. "Got to go open up downstairs anyway. Ava will be here any minute to start cooking."

He lingered for a brief moment to kiss her, and as Bull and Kaleb walked away towards the bikes, breathed quickly in her ear "There's an auction in Vegas on the twelfth, they're going to make me transport the new arrivals down there, with Cash. And I think Bull might have planted a bug under your coffee table."

She said nothing, but the slight flexing of her fingers against his arm told him the message had been received.

Liane waved as the bikes roared away, like a good little girlfriend, and then she said several swear words under her breath, turned around and ran quickly back up the stairs.

She was careful to make no sound as she moved through the apartment, lowering herself to the floor beside the coffee table and rolling to her back to look up at its underside.

The bug was small. Neat. Government issue, she suspected, but she didn't dare pull it out to examine it more closely. Instead she eased silently back, got up and went into the kitchen, her eyes narrowed. Where had Kaleb stood and what had he touched?

She found another bug in the fake pot plant on her kitchen windowsill. Bull hadn't been anywhere near it, so Kaleb had to have planted it. Which meant they were suspicious... she had to assume of her, since they seemed to trust Drew absolutely now, or they would never have let him see the group who were about to be trafficked into the country.

Government issue, she thought, and then she wondered, who's listening in on the other end?

Leaving the apartment as quietly as possible, she headed downstairs to let Ava into the kitchen and then told her cook she was going out for a little while. She was about to get in her truck when it occurred to her that might be bugged too. They might even have put a tracker on it.

"Shit and bollocks," she muttered fervently, before turning away from the truck and walking a few feet down the trail towards the lake she and Drew had taken on their first walk. She paused to listen, but there was nobody else in the car park this early and she couldn't imagine any of the Brethren laying in wait here just in case she happened to walk this way.

She'd retrieved her burner phone from its hiding place before leaving her apartment and pulled it out now. This close to the roadhouse, she could tap into her own WiFi and the VPN she had set up: it only took a couple of minutes to pull up an encrypted email address she'd created just for this purpose and send an email to Jessikah with all the latest information she had. Erasing the browser history and logging off, she put the phone away and pulled out her other phone, bringing up the secure messaging app she used to communicate with her bosses.

I may be compromised. Targets placed listening devices in my apartment this morning. Appear to be government issue.

She waited, and it wasn't long before a message came back.

This may present an opportunity to flush out the mole, by sharing some incorrect information.

"Are you freaking kidding me?" Liane muttered, thumbs dancing as she typed.

Trying anything like that will only confirm I'm a plant. I respectfully decline to risk my cover that way until it's time to exit. I have new information but it has to be held close as extremely sensitive. AFAIK Drew and I are the only ones outside the Brethren who know.

She'd made the decision the previous evening that she couldn't conceal that she knew the 'merchandise' coming in was human trafficking victims. They would need too much in the way of other resources ready to hand.

As she'd fully expected, her boss expressed shock over the human trafficking... and then basically said, Well it's not our problem, I'll pass it on to the FBI.

Liane took a deep breath, knowing she might be jeopardizing her career with her next words, but she typed them anyway.

While Bull indicated the mole is DEA, I don't trust anyone outside our agency. I think we should handle this.

This isn't your job. Leave it for the FBI.

I'm not prepared to sit back and let this happen, and neither is Drew. We'll be taking action. You need to back me up.

She could almost hear her boss spitting curses, but finally the response came back. I'll have an action team in the area on the 4th. You better get me some clear intel on exactly when and where, and be prepared to extract yourself and Murphy.

Thank you. You won't regret it.

Let's hope you don't, was the slightly ominous reply, and Liane winced before closing the app and putting her phone away, walking back towards the roadhouse with her shoulders slumped. A year of work, and she might be about to throw her career away, because if the bust didn't go absolutely perfectly, all of the agencies would be looking for a scapegoat and Liane knew exactly who that was going to be.

But she thought again of the look on Drew's face as he'd described those women and children in cages, the misery, fear and despair on their faces. The greedy lust on Kaleb's face as he'd looked at the little Chinese girl he'd selected.

And she knew there was no other way. This was the only choice to be made, no matter the price she or Drew might have to pay for it.

Chapter Seventeen

Drew finally discovered why his cousin had built such a nice new barn at his ramshackle cabin, when Bull sent him and Kaleb to 'get it ready for their guests'. The Brethren had probably paid for the damn thing, he thought, as he and Kaleb spread rubber mats around the floor and unstacked a pile of buckets, obviously meant to be makeshift toilets. Some odd fixtures he hadn't really noticed before made sense now, too; iron rings set into concrete floor at regular intervals presumably were meant to have chains and shackles bolted to them.

Cells were expensive to build, and while the facility in Edmonton was obviously being used to hold the captives for some time before they were moved on, from what Bull and Kaleb said they would only hold them in the barn for one night before heading to the auction in Vegas. Why go to all the expense and effort of building cells when you could just chain people like animals, after all?

Drew tasted blood, realized he'd bitten the inside of his lip. Huffing out a sharp breath, he forced himself to focus, used the breathing techniques he'd learned long ago. Practiced patience. He was good at patience. He'd once lain on a remote, rocky mountainside for five days, through blazing hot days and bitterly cold nights, for the chance to take a shot at a target it turned out had been killed by a drone strike a week earlier. At least this time, he was pretty sure he'd get to actually complete his mission.

"I'm heading out," Kaleb yelled from the door. "Going over to Gerry's to help him get ready there."

"Want me to come with you?" Drew tried not to sound too eager, but Gerry's house was still the one location neither he nor Liane had been able to identify. The Brethren were oddly secretive about it. Now he was a full member, he was hoping they'd clue him in.

“Nah,” Kaleb called back. “See you tomorrow.”

“Shit,” Drew muttered as Kaleb left. Trying to follow Kaleb would be pointless: he’d stick out like a sore thumb following along on the quiet country roads. With a sigh, he closed the barn door and looked around.

Might as well get my rifle and try some more target shooting. He’d been to the range a few times since going with Liane, getting accustomed to the Glock, and was definitely improving with it as he learned to compensate for only having one good eye. It made him feel confident that eventually, he could learn to shoot accurately with his rifle again.

He was walking up the steps to the cabin when a low whistle made him look around. He raised his brows in surprise as Jason Hunter slipped out from among the trees behind the cabin.

“Hello, stranger. You hang around in my woods a lot?” he greeted.

“Only when the trail cam I rigged up on your driveway alerts me a vehicle’s come in,” Jason deadpanned back, surprising him. “Wanted to check in, see how things are going. This is the first time you've been here alone, though."

Thinking of the bug placed in Liane's apartment, Drew waved Jason away from the cabin. The sheriff gave him a curious look, but followed along as Drew walked back into the woods, walking until the cabin and barn were out of sight.

"I went up to Edmonton a couple days ago," Drew began.

Jason's brows flew up as he listened, and his expression turned steadily grimmer. "Jesus," he said finally as Drew finished his report. "Human trafficking. Damn. That makes sense."

"In what way?"

"The Manhunters." Jason kicked at a loose rock on the ground, stuffing his hands in his pockets as he frowned in thought. "There are a few loose ends around that case that have never quite tied themselves off. You know the basics... that my uncle, along with a gang of cronies including my predecessor, were hunting people in the woods around

Woodvale, dumping the bodies in a bone pit in my uncle's back yard?"

Drew nodded. He'd been in hospital recovering from the first of several operations on his eye when the story broke, had seen plenty of news reports.

"There were eighty-six victims found in that bone bit, and six of them are still unidentified. All men. DNA racial profiling has come back that four are Asian - Cambodian, Thai and Chinese - and two are Hispanic."

"You think they were family members of some of the smuggling victims," Drew leaped to the obvious conclusion.

"Makes sense, doesn't it? Grown men aren't much use to people smugglers. Maybe you could sell them as some sort of slave labourers, but there can't be a huge market for them. And if they were troublemakers... very possible my uncle was happy to take them off the Brethren's hands." Jason shook his head, spat as if he had a bad taste in his mouth. "And this explains the other missing people. Our journalist friend Barry had been tracking disappearances for years, because too many people were going missing around this part of the state and none of them ever turned up again. Not all of them were in the bone pit. There's still about half a dozen people unaccounted for... and all of them are young women, including the state senator's niece whose disappearance got Barry interested in the first place. The FBI had their suspicions that there was another serial killer operating in the region, one targeting young women."

"Not a serial killer. Human traffickers. The Manhunters and the Brethren had some sort of mutual backscratching deal going on," Drew realized. "The Brethren took anyone of trafficking value, and the Manhunters got the rest."

"Now I think about it. Emily Darnell and Sasha Thoms are about the same age as Kaleb, they might well have been school classmates. They were on their way back from college in Boise, vanished from a rest stop. Their parents insisted they wouldn't have gone off with a stranger... but maybe they got in a car with someone they knew well. An old school friend."

"Served themselves up on a platter." Drew felt sick again just thinking about it.

"Young, white and pretty. They'd have fetched a good price in Vegas."

"Do you think they're still alive?"

"Maybe." Jason looked struck by the thought. "It's certainly possible. I'll talk to Carruthers, my FBI contact."

"At least we know their names," Drew said grimly. "I can hardly bear to think about all the others they've trafficked into God knows what hellish situations."

"Me neither. At least we can help the ones who are coming over the border soon. What about your local contact, the undercover agent? Has he reported to his bosses yet, and what's their plan?"

Of course, Drew realized, he hadn't had the opportunity to tell Jason who his contact was. He hesitated only a moment before revealing Liane's identity: he trusted Jason absolutely and knew the information would go no further. Wherever the leak in the DEA or FBI was, it predated Jason's arrival in the area anyway.

Jason blinked. "Liane… from the roadhouse?" He sounded incredulous. "She's the undercover agent?"

"ATF." Drew nodded. "She's been in place over a year."

"I would never have guessed it was her! Damn. She's a good actress." Jason looked distinctly impressed.

"She is. She's planning to fill in her bosses today, but she didn't seem particularly hopeful that they'd be enthused about intervening. Human trafficking isn't their area. She thinks they'll want to handball it to the FBI, but that carries risks because we still don't know for certain that the mole really is DEA. Or that there's only one mole."

"What a mess. Do you think they'll sit on their hands?"

"They might. Liane won't, and I definitely won't."

"So I'm guessing you'd like some backup?" Jason grinned, and in the slightly feral expression Drew saw the old hunger for action. He'd felt it rising in his own blood, the adrenaline build as the time for combat approached.

"I reckon we do it here." Drew pointed towards the barn. "Wait for them to bring all the captives in, chain them up, settle in to relax for the night. The only thing is I don't know exactly how many Brethren members there'll be: I don't know if the Canadian crew will be coming over the border and whether they'll stay over or not."

"Let me know if you can. I'll operate on the assumption that there may be a few extra hostiles."

"And if the ATF do decide they'll come to the party, I'll get them to reach out to you so you're not tripping over each other out here."

"Gotcha. Just as long as they don't try to keep me out of the action!"

Jason disappeared into the woods as silently as he'd appeared, and Drew shook his head with a touch of envy. He was pretty stealthy himself - he'd had to learn to be in order to get into position and stay hidden for days on end waiting to take his shot - but Jason Hunter was a ghost.

Making his way back to the cabin, Drew closed everything up before hopping on his bike. He needed to see Liane, tell her that he'd talked to Jason, though they'd have to do it away from the roadhouse. He still couldn't quite believe Bull had bugged Liane's apartment, but there was no other logical explanation - that Drew could come up with, anyway - for his odd action under the coffee table earlier.

They must suspect Liane, he thought as he rode back to Redstone Creek. They know there's definitely an undercover agent in town, but they don't know who. They must be going through a process of elimination; anyone who wasn't literally born in town who interacts with the Brethren on a reasonably regular basis. For some reason, they'd obviously dismissed any suspicions of Drew. Perhaps because he'd come to town after they'd been warned there was an agent in place, and because of his familial relationship with Jacob, who Bull and Kaleb at least had obviously liked and trusted completely. Drew knew he looked enough like Jacob that the bikers were obviously lulled into a false sense of security. It was hard to maintain distrust of someone who looked like a friend and acted exactly as they expected someone who shared their ideology to act. The old adage of if it looks like a duck, walks like a duck and quacks like a duck, it's most likely a duck. The shipment of drugs he and Kaleb had brought back from Canada getting to its destination without interception, trackers or even information arriving at the DEA that it was coming, was apparently the final thing that convinced Bull he could be trusted.

The roadhouse came into view and Drew eased off the throttle, turning into the parking lot and parking up in the Brethren's usual spot. There were no other bikes present, but he reminded himself that didn't necessarily mean nobody on the Brethren's payroll was present.

"Hey, stud," Liane called from behind the bar as he entered the roadhouse, and he walked straight back behind the bar and leaned in to kiss her.

"Hey, yourself."

“Back so soon? Just can’t stay away, huh?” She smiled up at him, teasing. Playing for their audience, which was half a dozen regulars on their stools at the bar, getting stuck into their early afternoon beers. “Hey, Joe, you got the bar for a bit? I want a few minutes with my man.”

“You got it, boss,” the other barman said cheerfully. “I can handle these idiots. You going upstairs?”

“Outside for some fresh air, I think. Been so busy, I don’t know the last time I went for a walk. C’mon, let’s take a stroll down to the lake.” She tucked her hand into the crook of Drew’s arm and he went with her willingly.

“You were right,” she said softly as they walked down the trail between the tall pines behind the roadhouse, the only sounds the birds singing in the trees and their boots crunching on dry pine needles. “Bull put a bug under the coffee table, and Kaleb planted another one in my kitchen.”

“I think it’s a fishing expedition. They know there’s an undercover agent and they’re going through a process of elimination.”

She snorted. “Expensive fishing expedition. Pretty sure the bug is government issue.”

Drew blew out his lips in a silent whistle. That added a new dimension. “Do you think someone is listening in live? Someone on the government’s payroll?”

“Maybe. I’m feeling very untrusting, I gotta tell you. I briefed my boss in on the trafficking victims incoming and he wanted to handball it to the FBI. I flat out refused and bullied him into agreeing to provide a strike team to back us up on the fourth.”

“We’ve got other help too,” Drew said, and filled her in on his conversation with Jason.

They reached the lake shore and stood by the small wooden jetty there, looking out over the blue waters. Boats bobbed about, more plentiful now the summer visitors were beginning to arrive. It was a picture-postcard scene, tranquil and beautiful, and Drew found it hard to believe that ugliness lurked so close by. So much of his active military service had been spent in harsh, unforgiving terrain, under the brutal desert sun or in amongst jagged, inhospitable mountain peaks. Spring and summer in northern Idaho felt deceptively peaceful and safe, but his life was just as much in peril now as it ever had been.

And so was Liane's, which made a very uncomfortable feeling settle in his gut. He'd served alongside women - while they hadn't been able to become Rangers until very recently, there were plenty of army regulars, drivers and logistics officers at all levels, plus helicopter and airplane pilots he'd worked with and respected, but he'd never gone into action with a woman he had feelings for at his side, and it went against every instinct he possessed.

"It's gotta be the lake," Liane said suddenly, which made him blink.

"Huh?"

"That has to be how the shipment on the fourth is coming in. And why they've picked that date." She pointed out at the water. "The northern part of the lake is in Canada, it crosses the border. Normally Border Patrol are pretty busy out here - they have a couple patrol boats - but on the fourth, it's on a

Saturday this year, the lake will be absolute chaos. Boats everywhere. If you have two that look basically identical, they could easily swap places in the middle of the lake. Hell, you could even swim people between two boats."

It made sense. A lot of sense. And it introduced a new dimension to what they would potentially have to deal with.

"That means someone from the Brethren has a boat," Drew said, thinking out loud. He'd been to just about everyone's home now, seen all their vehicles, cleaned them all too while he was in his probationary period. None of them lived on the lakeshore or along the creek that gave Redstone Creek its name, and he hadn't seen a boat on a trailer in anyone's garage or yard, either.

"You still don't know where Gerry lives, right?" Liane said what he was just thinking. "It's got to be him. He and Jacob always used to talk about going fishing together."

"Strangely enough, he hasn't asked me if I like fishing," Drew murmured.

"Maybe it's a euphemism. Nothing to do with fishing at all."

"I think you're onto something." The lake had to be the key. Drew had been struggling to work out why the Brethren were collecting the trafficking victims into a large group instead of slipping them across the border individually or in small groups. A boat with a good-sized below deck area, they could be packed in like sardines and transferred very quickly.

"I can't believe it's almost over," Liane said then, and he turned his head to look at her properly, since she was on his right side and he couldn't see her from his bad eye.

"Not even a week," he noted.

"I've been here so long." She rubbed at her arms, shaking her head. "I don't know what I'll do with myself, without a busy roadhouse to run."

"What happens to it when you're gone?"

She shrugged. "Not my problem. I've written references for my staff which will be posted to their home addresses, once this is all over. There's an email address on them to contact which will go to an ATF desk. No trace back to me personally, but they won't lose out."

Liane cared, Drew thought: cared about Merrick and Ava and Joe and the other staff. She'd poured a lot of herself into the roadhouse.

"What are you going to do, when it's over? Get another undercover assignment?"

She chewed on her lower lip before finally answering him. "No. I think I'm done. I've accumulated enough seniority to get a post anywhere I want in the agency. I just have to decide where."

She didn't ask his plans, Drew thought as they turned and started walking back along the trail to the roadhouse.

Maybe she instinctively sensed that he honestly didn't have any, beyond completing this mission and keeping her safe through it.

Chapter Eighteen

The Fourth of July dawned bright and sunny, barely a cloud in the sky, though there was the hint of smoke on the breeze as always from distant forest fires, Liane observed as she left her apartment and walked down the stairs. Drew walked ahead of her, and she knew from the tight set of his shoulders that the tension was getting to him. They'd both been dealing with the steady ratcheting up of pressure for days now, and they couldn't even talk about it for fear of the Brethren's bugs.

The Brethren were planning to come to the roadhouse for lunch and meet Drew there, so they knew nothing was going to happen this morning. Liane had already decided to close the roadhouse in the afternoon anyway;

from experience last year she knew that even her regulars tended to spend the day with their families and there wouldn't be a lot of business. Besides, she was going to be busy.

"Hey," she said quietly to Drew as they reached the door to the roadhouse and she pulled out her keys. "You doing okay?"

"Yeah. Calm before the storm, right?" He smiled at her, but she could tell it was forced. On impulse, she left her keys hanging in the lock, reached up to put her arms around his neck and pull him down to her, letting their foreheads touch.

"It's going to be okay," she whispered, trying to reassure herself as much as him. Trying to will the outcome she wanted into being.

His hands came up to clasp her waist, though he said nothing, just turned his head slightly to place a slow, lingering kiss on her lips.

Both of them knew, though neither had said anything, that this might be the last time they were ever alone like this. The last time they'd ever kiss, though Liane found herself fervently wishing it wasn't so, that somehow, once the action was all over, they could find each other again.

She just didn't think it was likely. She'd be going back to DC to debrief, and though she'd eventually probably have to come back to give evidence at whatever trials took place for the Brethren members, who knew where Drew would be by then? He'd have to leave the area too, and he hadn't mentioned any plans, only muttered something about Guàlize, of all places, and how there might be a possible job opportunity for him there.

"Be careful out there." His voice was a low rasp against her temple. "I don't think I could stand it if something happened to you."

"You'll be in more danger than I will. You be careful."

"Yes, ma'am."

A lump welled in her throat, and she had to close her eyes against the stinging tears that threatened. "Thank you," she whispered.

"What for?"

"Everything. Being here. Being you."

His lips caressed her brow, feather-light. “I couldn’t have gotten this far without you. I’m just blundering around in the dark, it’s a miracle I haven’t fucked up your op.”

Liane forced a laugh around her tight throat. “There wouldn’t be an op without your intel. Don’t sell yourself short. You’d make a great undercover agent.”

“Pretty sure none of the alphabet agencies would take me, with only one good eye.”

“They’d be fools to turn you down just because of that, and they’re not the only game in town anyway. If your thing in Guàlize doesn’t work out, get in touch. My sister’s working for a private outfit. They might very well have something for you.”

“I’ll keep it in mind.”

The sound of a car turning into the lot behind them made Liane step back, reluctantly. It was Merrick, arriving for his shift; Ava would already be in the kitchen doing lunch prep. Merrick nodded at them curtly as he came up to the door. He hadn’t warmed particularly to Drew, always giving his Brethren-branded vest the stink eye.

"I have to go. We're meeting at Bull's and then coming back here for lunch. I asked if I could just meet them here, but Bull said no." Drew spoke loudly enough for Merrick to hear, as Liane finished unlocking the front door and pushed it open. "Seems dumb, but when the boss says jump, we ask how high."

Merrick sneered, slipping past them into the bar, going to switch on the lights. Liane ignored him, reaching out to grasp Drew's hand briefly. She didn't want to let him go, some ancient instinct inside her warning not to. "Take care."

"You too." He squeezed her hand back, looking into her eyes. "It'll be alright, Liane."

She truly hoped so, but as she watched him walk away, mount his bike and roar off down the road, her guts were churning.

"It's just nervous anticipation," she whispered to herself, making herself look away from Drew's distant figure. "This is going to go like clockwork."

Not that any bust she'd ever participated in had gone precisely according to plan, of course, but she pushed that intrusive thought away and squared her shoulders. She had work to do.

Just before noon, the roadhouse door swung open to admit another party looking for lunch, or at least, that was what Liane assumed they were, until she recognized the man at the head of the group, Terrence Mallon, leader of an ATF strike team she'd worked with previously. His eyes met hers and widened.

You don't know me, Liane thought fiercely, glancing away as though entirely disinterested. And, what the fuck? Had her boss not warned the ATF strike team that she was here at the roadhouse? At least they weren't wearing identifying gear, but they couldn't have been more obviously law enforcement.

"Ain't got no more tables for lunch," Merrick informed Terrence blithely.

"What about that table?" one of the other members of the strike team pointed at the Brethren's table, not yet occupied.

"Reserved." Liane's tone was curt. "Sorry, folks. It's busy today. Can't help you out."

"Not sure I'd trust the food here anyway." Terrence didn't look at her as he spoke laughingly to his team. "Looks pretty grubby. C'mon, we'll pick up some sandwiches or something at the gas station and keep on going."

Get the hell out of here before the Brethren arrive, Liane thought at them fiercely. And she hoped they weren't driving the black SUVs which were standard government issue, either, because if the Brethren saw a pair of those close by, they might be spooked and call off the transfer.

"Who were they?" Merrick asked curiously as the door closed again.

"How would I know?" Liane feigned a disinterested shrug. "Ain't got time to worry about folks just passing through when we can't even feed them. Rude assholes, anyway. Probably wouldn't have left you much tip. Unlike the Andrades, so get over and take their order, kiddo." She pointed Merrick to where an older couple - regulars - were trying to get his attention.

Through the window, she saw Terrence, pausing by his vehicle - a gray SUV instead of a black one, fortunately - almost as though he expected her to come out and brief him. What an idiot. She was definitely going to take this up with her boss later.

On the other hand, she mused as she made drinks with her hands on autopilot, maybe her boss was just being cautious and compartmentalizing information. Information Liane herself had sent out had ended up being compromised, though that was before they knew for sure there was a mole at DEA. Still, it didn't mean there couldn't be a mole at ATF too. Not telling anyone exactly where she was located was another layer of protection for her. At this late stage, at least warning Terrence where to avoid would probably have been smart, though.

The Brethren came in, oddly without Gerry who was for some unexplained reason not present, ate their meal with more boisterous laughter and knowing smirks at each other than usual. They were all in high spirits, obviously anticipatory, though knowing what they were anticipating made Liane feel sick, and it was hard to smile as she took the stack of bills Cash put on the bar.

"Happy Fourth of July," she said in a cheery tone, and the gang secretary nodded.

"You too. Going to watch the fireworks on the lake later?"

"Sure. Was hoping Drew might be around?" She made it a question, but Cash shook his head.

"We've got business this afternoon. Sorry, girl."

"Bros before hoes, I get it." Her expression made it clear she didn't much like it.

Cash gave her an approving smile, though. "Keep that in mind, and you'll do just fine as Drew's old lady."

It took everything she had not to haul back and punch Cash in his smirking mouth. She just smiled tightly instead and put the money in the cash drawer. "No Gerry today?"

"Miss him, did ya?" Cash laughed coarsely as Liane twisted her mouth up in distaste. "He's busy. Gettin' some last minute things done before… this afternoon. Don't you worry, he'll be back in here tomorrow. I'll tell him you were asking after him."

I won't be here tomorrow, and you and Gerry will both be cooling your heels in jail. Liane wanted so desperately to say it, but she closed her lips over the words.

Drew paused on his way out to say a quiet farewell, leaning across the bar to brush his lips against hers. He was doing a good job of appearing relaxed, she thought, despite knowing he was heading into an unknown situation where any number of unpredictable variables could endanger the outcome they hoped for.

"Take care," was all she dared say.

"You too." They exchanged one last glance before he followed the others out.

She closed the roadhouse at three sharp, telling a few folks who were reluctant to drink up and depart that it was her holiday too and they could shove off. Regulars used to her abrasive tongue, they laughed and quit the place quickly enough. Paying her staff and putting the rest of the day's takings in the safe, she ran the totals from the credit card machine on autopilot, half-laughing at herself when she realized it didn't matter. She'd never set foot inside the place again.

Locking the doors, she headed upstairs, took a quick shower and changed into practical cargo pants, hiking boots, a long-sleeved shirt and a light jacket. Checking and holstering her gun, she put three extra filled magazines into her pockets, collected her burner phone and glanced around the apartment.

She'd never kept anything here she couldn't live without. Any truly personal items were in storage in the attic at her mother's house, or in her personal effects locker at ATF headquarters in DC. She'd accumulated a few things over the last year she liked, though there was nothing here she'd truly regret leaving behind.

Nothing except Drew, that was.

With a wry smile, Liane closed the door behind her and headed down the stairs, making for her truck. She planned to log onto the ATF secure app and find out where to rendezvous with Terrence's field team.

Her hand was on the door handle when flashing red and blue strobe lights reflecting against the truck's windows made her turn. A sheriff's department vehicle screeched into the lot, the driver slamming the brakes on as the car pulled up at an angle beside her. Jason Hunter leaped out, his face pale.

"We've got a problem."

Chapter Nineteen

Drew worked on keeping his breathing steady and even as he rode his Harley along at the rear of the group, like the junior member he was. Bull's phone had rung as they left the roadhouse, and Bull's expression had darkened as he listened to whoever was calling, until he hung up abruptly.

"Change of plan," he barked. "We're heading directly to Gerry's place now. Fall in."

I'm finally getting to see Gerry's place, Drew thought, wishing he could update Liane. He might get a chance later. Though he wouldn't do so using the phone the Brethren had given him, he might be able to get away and use the burner phone Liane had provided. He'd found a way to hide it on his bike, having attached a magnet to the underside of the engine mount and a small metal box which held the phone to that.

The group rode through Redstone Creek and out the other side, turning off onto a side road that followed the creek that curved away from the southern side of the lake. A few minutes later Bull led them through another turn, this time onto an overgrown track which nonetheless showed signs of regular traffic passing through. It had once been a proper paved road, Drew thought as his bike bumped over cracked asphalt, moss and grass growing up through the breaks. The pine trees ubiquitous to the area grew close beside the road, making it hard to see.

They broke out of the pines and Drew's eyes widened in surprise at the size of the complex of buildings in front of them. This was not the single cabin he'd expected, or even a house; this was industrial, if dilapidated.

A timber mill, he thought, looking at the layout. An old one, one which had probably used the convenient geography of the creek to float timbers downstream from the lake. It had been closed for years, from the looks of things, maybe decades, but at least one of the buildings looked better maintained. The Brethren pulled their bikes up in front of it and shut them off, the rumbling engines dying away into complete silence. Drew couldn't even hear birds singing.

The building looked more like a house than the others, he thought; maybe a former supervisor's residence. He supposed someone would have had to live on site. And obviously, Gerry lived here now, as a door swung open and the biker stepped out onto the porch.

Gerry looked as pissed off as Bull had been; maybe he was the one who'd made that phone call. Drew wondered what it was all about, as he removed his helmet and set it on the seat of his bike.

"You," Gerry spat, pointing at him.

"What?" Drew wasn't going to take a step back for this punk. He jutted his jaw pugnaciously and glared him down instead.

Gerry stepped to the edge of the porch and threw something at Drew's feet. He looked down instinctively, frowning in puzzlement as he tried to make sense out of the mangled bits of metal and plastic.

"What's that?"

"Don't give me that shit! It's a fucking motion-sensitive trail camera. And I found it pointing at your driveway."

Fuck. Hunter's camera.

Not for an instant did Drew let anything other than confusion show on his face. Kaleb was turning to stare at him with an expression of pure betrayal; Bull looked furious, Cash calculating.

"What the hell's that got to do with me?" If he showed weakness, they'd tear him apart. His only hope was to sow doubt and division. "You don't think I fucking put it there?" Drew let outrage show in his face and voice. "What the fuck are you accusing me of, Gerry?" He took a menacing step forward.

"Did you put it there?" Kaleb asked suddenly, and to Drew's astonishment, the kid was looking at Gerry, not him. "You've never liked Drew. Are you trying to pull this bullshit to frame him or something?"

Gerry's face turned purple, and he swelled up like a bullfrog. He jumped down from the porch and went to grab Kaleb, but Drew stepped in the way.

"Leave Kaleb out of it. Your problem's with me."

"Fucking right it is," Gerry spat at him. "I've smelled a rat with you from the beginning. You talk about Jacob like the sun shone out his ass, but when he was drunk he used to talk about what a prissy little bitch you were as a kid. Said you were best buddies with some damn chink kid."

"Bullshit," Drew said, but he could sense the mood shifting. He thought Cash, at least, had been wavering, wondering if Gerry might have planted the camera. Now they were all looking at him with doubt in their expressions. "If you didn't plant that camera, someone else fucking did, because I've never seen it before in my life." That should have have the benefit of ringing true, because it was the truth. He'd known of its existence, but nothing more than that.

"Who'd be watching your place and only your place?" Gerry spat at him. "I checked around everyone's houses. No cameras anywhere."

"Why would I watch my own driveway?" Drew tried to sound logical. "If I wanted to watch my security, I'd put a camera on the house. Not the driveway."

"But if you wanted to watch who came and went, you'd put it on the driveway."

Gerry was glaring at him, toe to toe. Drew refused to back down.

"Whoever put the camera there," Bull said, breaking the deadlock. They both looked at him. "If it wasn't you, or someone you're reporting to..."

"The only person I report to is you!" Drew kept up his facade of injured innocence.

Bull scowled at him. "Shut up. I'm talking. Whoever put it there was watching your place. Which means we absolutely can't take the merchandise there. We need to move it direct from here... today."

"And he can't be involved." Gerry jabbed his finger into Drew's chest.

It was pure instinct: Drew's hand snapped up without him even consciously thinking about it. Half a second later Gerry was hopping backward, screaming, as Drew bent his finger back at an unnatural angle.

"Touch me again and I'll feed you that damn finger!" Drew snapped.

"Let him go!" Bull shouted, starting forward.

It was from the other side, his blind side, the threat came, though. Drew heard the whooshing sound of displacing air but wasn't quick enough to evade; he had to turn his head too far, only had time for his good eye to catch sight of the piece of four-by-four Cash was swinging. Right before it connected with the back of his head.

"Is there a problem, sheriff?" Liane said, stalling.

"Yes." Hunter gave her a direct look. "I know who you really work for, which is why I've come to you. Drew Murphy's in trouble."

She stiffened. “He only just left a few minutes ago. What’s happened?”

“With the Brethren?”

“Of course.” Dread lodged in the pit of her stomach.

“I put a trail camera on his driveway, to keep an eye on comings and goings… largely so I’d know when I could catch him there alone to talk. Someone found it about an hour ago.” He thrust his phone towards her: she looked unwillingly down at the screen. Swallowed bile as she easily recognized the man on the short, grainy piece of footage which played.

“That’s Gerry. The club sergeant-at-arms.” He was clearly captured in the moments before the camera was yanked off its mounting and the clip abruptly ended.

“Whoever they think put the camera there - Drew or someone else - they know the location is compromised.”

“Which means the team I called in are in the wrong place!” Liane groaned. She didn’t blame Hunter for placing the camera, not out loud at any rate; she could see from his sick expression he was already blaming himself anyway. “No way will they take the trafficking victims there now. They might abort the whole mission.”

“Maybe, but if you and Drew were correct about how they’re being transported, they might not. The Canadians might already be on the water.”

“Too late to tip off Border Force?” Liane wondered.

“Probably just too many boats out on the lake. There’s been a steady stream of boats on trailers heading this way all day. Unless we have more information about specifics on what boats they’re looking for - and the certainty that whoever we tip off isn’t on the Brethren’s payroll…”

“Yeah, and we don’t have that. At least a couple of the local Border Force officers pretty much have to be dirty.” Liane paced, thinking. “I need to call this in to my boss, get the team redeployed. See if maybe we can salvage the mission.”

"And get Drew out of there, because at best it's fifty-fifty whether they believe he didn't know about the camera. But where?"

They stared at each other.

"I don't know," Liane admitted. "We never did figure out where Gerry lives, and we think he's the one with the boat."

"Did you put a tracker on Drew?"

"No, we were worried they'd find it. They're surprisingly tech-savvy, and well-equipped - the bugs they planted in my apartment were good quality, recent government issue. And they insisted Drew have a low-tech phone. No GPS. Although..." Thinking about it, Liane grabbed for her own phone. Maybe Drew had the burner she'd given him with him, somehow. Or Jessikah could track the low-tech phone from the signals it bounced off cell towers, as she'd promised she could. Give them at least a general area to work in, and she and Hunter might be able to narrow it down from there.

"That phone's about six miles south of you," Jessikah's calm voice said down the phone about five minutes later. "Hasn't moved in the last half hour, but before that it was at your roadhouse. All night…"

"Yeah, thanks, Jess," Liane said hurriedly. "I have to go…"

"Call me back before you go in," Jessikah ordered. "I'll tap into a satellite and I can give you real-time operational support."

Once again, Liane was left wondering just what the hell kind of operation her sister was now working for: that was NSA-level access but a private company? She shoved the question aside, for now, already dialing another number, preparing to give her boss the bad news.

"We'll go in ahead," she said. "We're a lot closer."

"You and this local sheriff?"

She could hear the cynical distaste in her boss's voice.

"Me and the ex-Ranger," she corrected, "who knows these woods like the back of his hand."

Jason Hunter gave her a quick, sidelong glance, but he was already at the trunk of his car, yanking out and donning body armor. He held a vest out in her direction and she took it gratefully.

"You did your homework on me." He said it like a question.

"My sister did, actually. She's my tech support... because I haven't quite trusted the agency. When Drew told me you recruited him, I thought I'd best check you out. Wanted to be sure you weren't going to blunder in on my operation."

"And I have." Hunter looked disgusted with himself. "Can't believe they found that trail cam. I should have pulled it, but I thought, just one more day..."

"I think it was just sheer bad luck," Liane consoled as she fastened the Velcro tabs at the side of the vest. It was a little big for her, but a lot better than nothing.

Hunter was pulling guns from the trunk of his car; a pump-action shotgun and an MP5. He gestured that Liane should take her pick. She considered it and accepted the shotgun. It looked more menacing than her pink Glock, at least.

Hunter had jumped in the car, was pulling up a satellite view of the address Jessikah had given them on the dashboard computer. “The old mill,” he murmured to himself as Liane slid in alongside him. “That was abandoned back when I was a kid. We used to hang out and goof off there sometimes, me and some buddies. Good place to disappear and drink beer and nobody would have a clue where we’d gone.”

“Probably not a good idea to head up the driveway with sirens wailing,” Liane noted.

“Nah. We’ll go in here.” He touched another narrow road which ran parallel to the mill’s driveway, perhaps a half-mile distance. “Go in on foot. We’ll be on target by the time your strike team catch up. Unless they’ve got a helicopter?”

“I doubt it. My boss would have said something.”

“Gotcha.” He started the engine and peeled out of the lot, flicking on the roof lights but leaving the siren off, for now at least. “Hold tight.”

Chapter Twenty

"Fucking ouch." Drew regained consciousness with a start, groaning as he tried to move and his head responded with a twinge of agonizing pain. For a horrifying moment he thought he'd lost the sight in his left eye as well, as he blinked and it briefly didn't focus, but slowly the world became sharper again and he could see.

He was lying on the floor in a small, dark space. Bare concrete underneath him, gray cinderblock walls. The only light a bare bulb hanging from the ceiling.

And, he realized as he tried to move, his hands were tied behind him. Zip-tied, he discovered, exploring with his fingertips and feeling the plastic. But thin zip ties, not proper flex cuffs.

“Idiots,” he said aloud, before he pushing himself up, rolling to his knees. He didn’t bother getting to his feet yet, just leaned forward, tensed his muscles and slammed his wrists down against the small of his back sharply, forcing them apart. The zip tie snapped on the first try.

Getting to his feet, Drew felt gingerly at his head. There was a pretty hefty lump behind his ear which shot another blinding jolt of pain through him when he touched it, and his fingers came away sticky with blood, but it felt like it had pretty much stopped bleeding, the blood thick and clotted. He was going to have one hell of a headache, but he didn’t think his skull was fractured.

Even if it was, it wasn’t like he could do anything about it right now. He’d clearly been dumped wherever this was and locked in. The single door he could see looked depressingly solid, actual metal, and there was no handle on the inside. He gave it a couple of exploratory kicks, but thought he was more likely to break an ankle than the door, particularly as he could see it was meant to hinge inwards.

“Plan B,” Drew muttered, turning a circle and examining the room. He wondered if he was still on the mill property somewhere. He didn’t feel like all that much time had passed since Cash knocked him out, but he supposed he could be completely wrong. It wasn’t like there were any windows to let in light so he could assess what time of day it was.

Only three of the windowless walls of whatever building he was in were cinderblock; the other was drywall. He knocked experimentally, nodding thoughtfully at the hollow sound. Well, at this point he had nothing much left to lose. He took a step back, set himself, and smashed a side kick into the drywall.

It took only a few seconds for him to kick through two layers of board into the void beyond and rip enough away to make a hole big enough for him to scramble through. What he found on the other side stopped him dead, his mouth opening in shock.

Two young women - girls really, he doubted either were out of their teens - clung to each other in the far corner of the room, terrified expressions on their faces as they stared at him clambering through the wall.

Drew took in the room with a comprehensive glance. A stained double mattress on a basic iron bedframe with a few blankets on top. A bucket in the opposite corner. A cardboard box on the floor beside the bed, plastic water bottles visible in it; a small pile of dirty paper plates beside that. Another steel door the only apparent way out.

“Who are you?” one of the girls quavered. “Wh-what do you want?”

There was no defiance in either of them, only terror. The clothes they were wearing were little more than rags, and they were both barefoot, dirty and far too thin.

“My name’s Drew Murphy,” he said, “and I want what you want.”

They stared at him.

“To get the hell out of here.”

"You're one of them," the girl who hadn't spoken yet said accusingly.

She was looking at his vest, Drew thought, and he smiled wryly, shrugging the cut off and tossing it on the floor. He didn't need to pretend any more.

"Not really. I'm undercover, working for the sheriff's department."

"Sheriff McCarthy?"

"No. Pretty sure he was in their pocket, but he was one of the Manhunters... you don't know who that is, do you? How long have you been here?"

They both shrugged.

"A long time," the one who'd first spoken said. She seemed slightly the braver of the two, trying to shield her friend behind her. A little taller and sturdier with fair hair and blue eyes, Drew thought she was probably very pretty under all the dirt. Or would be, if her eyes weren't so haunted. "I'm Sasha."

"What?" He knew that name! "Sasha Thoms? And you... are you Emily Darnell?"

Emily cringed back further behind Sasha. Her hair was darker, a medium-brown, and she was even thinner than Sasha, on the verge of emaciation.

“Why have they kept you?” Drew wondered aloud, unable to understand why the Brethren hadn’t just sold the two girls on in Vegas, as he and Hunter had speculated they might.

“We know Kaleb.” Sasha answered him, her expression clouding over. “He… offered us a lift. The bus was so slow, and there was this really creepy dude on it who kept trying to hit on Emily, so we said yes. Only he didn’t take us home, he brought us here, to this abandoned mill. There were several others here. Kaleb said he’d found some bonus extra merchandise, but that older one - his uncle, I think…”

“Bull,” Emily said in a near-whisper.

“Yeah, he was furious. He said we couldn’t be sold on because we could identify them. We knew the location of this place and Kaleb’s name. It could compromise the whole operation. I think Bull planned to just kill us, but Gerry... Gerry said he'd like to keep us a while."

Emily shuddered, a full-body shudder, and Drew clenched his teeth and thought about all the ways he would like to make Gerry suffer.

"And you've been locked up here ever since?" he asked gently, prowling around the room to examine it quickly, checking the door even though he suspected it would be the same type of immovable construction as the one in the room he'd woken up in.

"Yeah." Sasha was still doing most of the talking. "Sometimes Gerry takes one of us over to his place for a shower. We've looked for opportunities to escape, but..."

"You don't even have shoes," Drew pointed out when she trailed off. "How far could you get, barefoot? We're several miles out of town, in rough country." Frankly he thought they were both lucky to still be alive, despite obviously having suffered horrible abuse at Gerry's hands, and quite probably other Brethren members.

Emily was watching him with untrusting eyes, but Sasha took a small step towards him.

"Yes! We couldn't. And even if I could - I couldn't leave Ems."

"Of course not," he agreed, grasping the end of the bedframe and giving it an experimental shake. It creaked but seemed basically sound, so he stepped up onto the mattress.

"What are you doing?" It was Emily who asked this time, a little curiosity creeping into her expression as she looked at him standing on the bed.

"I'm not keen on waiting around for the gang to get back and come through that door, or the other door, looking to finish me off." He reached above his head and knocked on the ceiling. "When you went to Gerry's place for a shower, did either of you get a good look at this building when you were coming back? Any chance you could describe the roof for me?"

"Sheet iron," Sasha said, hope beginning to creep into her eyes. "A fairly shallow pitch. Are you thinking we might get out that way?"

"Maybe. Unless you've designed a building specifically to keep people in, the roof's often the weak spot. I can hear this is just drywall sheeting fixed to the rafters. Should be able to smash through it and get into the roof space - and from there, we might be able to force off some of the sheet iron." He hopped off the bed again, pushed the mattress off it and wrenched a slat off the base. "Let's see what we can do, eh?"

It didn't take him long to break up the ceiling enough to make a hole they'd be able to get through. Sasha bravely stepped forward.

"I can go up and look, if you give me a boost."

"That's real brave of you, but I'll go."

"Don't leave us!" Emily's voice trembled as Drew gathered himself and jumped, grabbing hold of one of the rafters he'd exposed.

"I'm not leaving you." He pulled himself up into the hole in the ceiling. "If I can get this roof loose, I'm pulling you both up and we're all leaving together. Why don't you see if you can tear up one of those blankets and wrap some pieces around your feet, give them some sort of protection?"

Liane couldn't believe how fast and quietly Hunter moved through the woods. He seemed almost to glide over the ground, moving at a slow but steady jog, near-soundless. In contrast, twigs seemed to crack under her boots with every step even though she was trying to watch her footing. He didn't look back to check whether or not she was keeping pace, and she could tell he was desperately worried about Drew. Feeling guilty, she suspected, for having sent him into this situation and then accidentally compromised his safety when the camera was found.

She didn't try all that hard to keep up. Hunter was obviously more than competent enough to handle anything he might come across, and she had the satellite view of the mill's grounds up on her phone and her sister on the end of the line, talking into her earbud - and thank goodness she'd had her wireless earbuds in her purse.

"Another fifty yards and you'll be coming out of the trees," Jessikah said quietly in her ear. "I've got live satellite footage now: no sign of any movement on the property. Can't see any vehicles either but there are so many buildings, one of them could be a garage with a dozen vehicles in it and I wouldn't know."

"Any sign of a boat?" Liane asked, keeping her voice low.

"Nothing in the immediate vicinity. There's a dock in the creek and what might be a boathouse alongside, so again, might be something undercover that I can't see. I'll warn you if I see any approaching water traffic."

"Got it." Liane saw the break in the trees now. She didn't see Hunter until he made a soft sound to attract her attention; he was hunkered down between two small shrubby bushes, barely visible until she was practically on top of him.

"Jessikah says there's nobody moving around," she told him softly, crouching beside him.

“Big place to clear, just the two of us.” Hunter clearly didn’t like the situation one bit. “Any word on how far out your strike team are?”

“Another thirty minutes.”

Hunter chewed on his lower lip. “We could wait. But I’ve got a bad feeling.” He cast a quick grin her way. “Highly unscientific, but the last time my gut was churning like this, my uncle turned out to be a serial killer.”

She huffed a soft laugh, but she knew what he meant. She was trying to keep the intrusive thoughts at bay, but her imagination kept supplying horrific images of what could be happening to Drew in one of those buildings right now.

“You might not have thirty minutes,” Jessikah said in her ear. “A boat just split off from the gathering in the middle of the lake and is heading back your way. It’s a few miles away yet but moving at a decent speed; I’d say ETA maybe twenty minutes.”

Liane relayed the information to Hunter quickly. “If that’s some of the Brethren coming back after making the pickup, that might mean they aren’t all here. They’re divided. If we can take the place before they get here..."

"Divide and conquer." Hunter nodded. "The buildings on the northern side of the compound look a lot more dilapidated." He pointed, finger describing an arc. "What say we make an executive decision and focus on those over here?"

"That one looks like a house." Liane pointed in the opposite direction. "Site supervisor's residence maybe, when the place was in operation?" It was set slightly away from the main mill itself, and looked in better condition. "Start there? My guess is that's where Gerry actually lives."

"You take the back. I'll get the front."

He was giving her the safer approach, she recognized, with the opportunity to stay within the cover of the treeline until the latest possible moment. But considering his apparent stealth abilities - and presumably, his far greater experience in combat as a Ranger - Liane was perfectly prepared to follow his lead.

They split up, Jason vanishing silently into the maze of dilapidated buildings, Liane picking her way as quietly as she could through the thinning pine trees at the forest's edge. She hadn't reached the house when a loud noise had her spinning around, staring in the direction of one of the smaller buildings which was apparently being demolished from the inside out, as a large piece of its roof slid off and crashed to the ground.

A bellow of "What the hell, Murphy!" from the house had her running. If Drew was in that building, she wanted to make sure she got there before anyone else.

Chapter Twenty-One

The roof was fairly sturdy, but it wasn't built to withstand force being applied from the inside. Drew braced himself against the rafters and shoved up with his back in one corner, and a big piece of the iron sheeting just popped right off and slid to the ground with a tremendous crash.

"Shit!" That would bring someone running. He leaned down over the hole in the ceiling, reaching his hand down. "Quick, come on, before someone comes!"

Emily was clearly reluctant to touch him, but Sasha urged her up onto the bed. "Hold your hand up, go on, I'll be right behind you!"

Neither of them weighed anything like as much as they should, he discovered as he hauled them up one after the other. His head spun a little as he got to his feet again, and he had to grab onto the exposed edge of the roof sheeting to steady himself.

“I can hear shouting,” Sasha said, peering out of the hole in the roof. “And there’s someone running this way. With a gun.”

“Stay down.” Drew didn’t want to push her, so he gently pressed at the side of her upper arm. “Don’t make yourself a target. I’m going to go down there and deal with whoever that is.”

“I think it’s a woman.” Sasha obligingly crouched down, but kept peering out of the hole. “I’ve never seen a woman here before. Is she with you?”

“Maybe,” though he didn’t know how Liane might have figured out where he was. He took another quick look around. “I’m going to help you both down, and then you and Emily run for the trees, over there, see? It’s not far.”

“And what will you be doing?” Emily asked, her voice quiet as she stared at him with wide eyes.

"Holding off any pursuit." Though without weapons, he wasn't sure exactly how. Hopefully, it really might be Liane out there. "Come on. Let's go." Scrambling through the hole in the roof, he lowered himself and dropped to the ground. "Jump, Sasha!"

He could see the fear on her face, but she jumped bravely, and Emily waited only long enough for Drew to catch Sasha and set her on her feet before following.

"Run!" Drew pointed, and the two girls clasped hands and ran as fast as they could, away from the shouting which was getting steadily closer.

A shotgun blast made Drew start, and then he heard Liane's voice yelling his name.

"Here!" he called, trying to keep his voice low, not wanting to alert the enemy to his position.

A second later Liane rounded the corner of the building, her eyes scanning him up and down in a quick assessment before obvious relief crossed her face.

"You look like hell," was what she said, however. "There's blood all down your neck."

"Got smacked upside the head with a plank," Drew summarized. "I'll be okay."

"If you say so." She looked magnificent, wearing a bulletproof vest with SHERIFF emblazoned across it, cargo pants and boots. A pump-action shotgun in her hands completed the badass look.

"Where'd the vest come from?" Drew nodded towards it.

"Hunter. He turned up not long after you left, realizing his trail camera had been found. He's out there somewhere. Who did I just see running for the trees?"

A bullet pinged off the wall just beyond them, making Drew and Liane both duck for cover.

"Two girls Gerry's been keeping captive. We've got to get them out of here. One of them's in a pretty bad way, and neither of them have any shoes. I doubt they can run far."

"The ATF strike team is fifteen minutes out." Liane touched an earpiece in one ear, made a face. "Unfortunately, we don't have that long. Jessikah's watching via a satellite in real time, and she says there's a boat maybe five minutes away."

A gunshot cracked not too far away, followed by a loud cry, and then silence.

"I got him," Hunter's voice called a moment later. "He was trying to creep up on you guys."

Liane gestured, and Drew nodded. They both ran towards the sound of Hunter's voice, keeping in a low crouch.

They found Hunter standing by the porch of the house, looking down at a body. It was Ed, the oldest and slowest of the Brethren; he'd presumably been left behind to keep an eye on things. His gun lay on the floor not far from his hand. Drew stooped to scoop it up. A Walther PPK, it at least looked clean and well-maintained, and when he checked the magazine, it was full.

"Y'all okay?" Hunter scanned Drew up and down, grimacing. "Sorry about the trail camera."

"Not your fault. Just shitty luck Gerry saw it. He's been looking for something on me."

"Surprised they didn't just off you outright, to be honest."

Liane drew in a sharp breath. Drew reached for her instinctively, putting his free hand on her arm.

"They didn't have concrete proof I knew about its existence. I insisted I hadn't put it there, which had the advantage of being the truth, and I'm pretty sure they were split on believing me. They shoved me in their little lockup and probably planned to try and interrogate me properly when they got back. I wasn't going to hang around."

"Boat's coming in now," Liane relayed. "Do you think Ed had time to call and tell them you were breaking out and he had trouble?"

All three of them looked down at the dead biker on the ground. His phone was nowhere in evidence.

"Either yes, and they're expecting us, or no, and we might get the drop on them," Hunter said. "Whichever it is, we can't just leave. Not considering how many hostages they've now presumably got on that boat."

They could hear the boat engine now, being gunned hard as it approached the dock. Drew suspected that was a bad sign, that the Brethren were in a hurry because Ed had indeed managed to call them. He jerked his head to Hunter, who nodded back.

“I found Sasha Thoms and Emily Darnell. They’re hiding in the trees. Kaleb picked them up and thought to add them into the trafficking pool, but didn’t realize it was a problem because they could identify him. Gerry decided to keep them and presumably they’ve been here ever since.”

Hunter’s eyes popped, but he nodded again. “Well, that explains why they weren’t in the Manhunters’ pit, eh?”

“What’s our plan?” Liane asked. The three of them had, by unspoken agreement, moved away from Ed’s body and slipped around one of the derelict buildings, angling to get a clear view to the dock and the boat just tying up there.

“We have to get them away from the boat - and the potential hostages - and keep them busy until your ATF strike team get here to help with the arrests," Drew said.

"Yeah, while I could try yelling county sheriff, you're all under arrest, I suspect they're not going to back down unless faced with overwhelming firepower." Hunter's grin was wry. "Plus, I don't have enough handcuffs."

Drew snorted with laughter, though he checked himself at the sight of Liane's pale face. She wouldn't get the kind of gallows humor the Rangers often resorted to in these last, tense moments before combat. "We all know that some of them aren't going to surrender under any circumstances, right?" he asked her, keeping his voice soft.

"Yeah." Her jaw was tight, but her eyes were steady as she met his gaze. "Don't worry. I've pulled the trigger with a human target in my sights before, and I'll do it again when I have to. I'm sure not going to cry for any of those bastards afterwards."

"Atta girl." Hunter gave a sharp nod.

"Murphy!" It was a deep-throated, enraged roar. Bull, Drew thought.

"They're looking for him," Liane said, quick and soft. "We'll draw them away from the boat. Hunter, you get on board and secure the hostages. Take the boat back out on the water, if you can, so they can't get back on it."

"Yes, ma'am." He slipped away like a ghost, vanishing into the shadows between buildings almost instantly.

"What the hell, look at that roof!" another voice shouted nearby.

"That's on the girls' side! Did he get them out too? Ed! Ed, where the hell are you?" A jangling of keys. They were going to unlock one of the doors to the makeshift prison, Drew thought, and gestured to Liane to stay where she was, but move along the side of the building. She nodded silently, pointing forward then holding up three fingers before lowering her hand to grasp her gun, finger slipping inside the shotgun's trigger guard.

Three in front of them, Drew deduced, wishing he had an earpiece as well. That meant at least four others somewhere else, and that was assuming none of the Canadian Brethren had come back with the locals.

An assumption he certainly wasn't going to make.

"I don't have a good view," Jessikah warned in Liane's ear. "The satellite's at an oblique angle. I'm losing them in between the buildings."

"It's okay," Liane whispered back. "Just give me what you can. They can't have any idea you're watching."

"Just don't get shot, big sis." For the first time, tension entered Jessikah's voice. Liane imagined her sister sitting at her desk, probably in a comfortable leather chair, screens illuminating the space around her. "I want to meet that sexy Ranger of yours."

Across the alleyway between the two buildings they were creeping between, Liane glanced at Drew. He really was sexy as hell, she allowed, even roughed up with dried blood all down the side of his head and neck. He moved with lethal grace and purpose, gaze sweeping continuously for danger both ahead and behind.

“Drew!” That was Kaleb’s voice, Liane thought. “Brother, what’s going on? I believe you didn’t know about the trail cam - we only locked you in because we had to go to the pickup, didn’t have time to talk to you properly about it!”

“Bullshit,” Drew mouthed, his expression cynical as he reached up to finger the dried blood around the gash on his head. Liane nodded.

“We gotta find those girls,” another voice said, lower and closer, just around the corner, Liane thought. “If they make it to the road and get picked up, we’re up shit creek. They know too much.”

“We’ll find them. They can’t have gone far. The bikes are all still here. They’re probably hiding in the buildings.” That was Gerry’s voice, angry and arrogant. She heard boots crunching on the rough ground, tensed herself and raised her shotgun.

“ATF,” she said loudly, stepping around the corner, seeing from the corner of her eye Drew dart across the gap to cover her targets from a different angle. "You're under arrest. Put your weapons on the ground and your hands on your head."

Gerry's mouth was open with shock, as was Cash's, standing beside him. They both stared at her with wide, disbelieving eyes.

"You?" Gerry gasped out.

"Me." Liane smiled tightly. "It's been me all along, you filthy little creep. Now drop it." They both had guns in hand, but only Cash looked half-ready to use his, Gerry's dangling from slack fingers.

"And fucking you," Gerry spat at Drew. "ATF, I knew you were a dirty rat."

"Nah, I'm not a fed." Drew shook his head. "She's the one calling the shots." He inclined his head towards Liane, though his gun never twitched so much as an inch away from his targets.

"Then she's the one who's going to have to die first," a new voice said behind them, and Liane swore, spinning to face the new threat. Bull had somehow crept quietly into the back end of the alley behind them, and he fired before she could bring the shotgun to bear, before darting back around the corner.

"Ah!"

Even wearing a ballistic vest, getting shot hurt like a son of a bitch. The bullet hit her just below the solar plexus, flinging her backwards, and she crashed to the ground. The shotgun went off and she only had time to hope like hell she hadn't hit Drew before the world went gray around the edges and she briefly blacked out.

Chapter Twenty-Two

"Liane!" Drew threw himself at the ground as both Cash and Gerry fired; their shots went high, over his head. He fired back, but they were both already running. He heard a yelp, though, and suspected he'd grazed one of them. Rapidly, he belly-crawled to Liane's side, scrambled up, grabbed her under the armpits and dragged her through a gaping hole in the crumbling wall of the building beside them, taking what little cover he could find.

"Ow, fuck." She woke up quickly, groaning, feeling at her chest. "Yes. Jess, I'm okay."

She was talking to her sister, he realized, as she pushed herself to a sitting position.

"Didn't hit you, did I?" she checked.

“Nah, your shot went pretty much straight up as you fell. Little rain of lead shot fell on Cash and Gerry, distracted them while they were trying to shoot me, so it did some good.”

“Murphy!” That was Gerry’s bellow; Drew grimaced. He’d hoped for a few seconds more respite.

“How far out is your strike team?” he asked quietly.

“Jess says six minutes, and they’re coming in hot. We just have to keep them busy and pinned down until then.” Heaving herself to her feet, Liane chambered another round in the shotgun with a wince of pain.

“I’m gonna carve your other fucking eye out!” Gerry again.

“Distraction,” Drew mouthed, pointing to the other side of the building. He’d seen the slightest flicker of movement through the gaps in the boards there. He pointed to the shotgun in Liane’s hands, mimed pulling the trigger, and pointed to the movement again.

Liane nodded. Firmed her jaw. Aimed, and fired.

They both ran, not hanging around once their location had been pinpointed by the shotgun blast, and it was the right call as a hail of gunfire smashed through the broken timber right where they'd been standing. Someone was screaming on the other side of the building, though, and Drew shared a vicious grin with Liane. The shotgun pellets had done their job.

"Incoming on the other side of the building," Jessikah said sharply in Liane's ear. "You're about to be surrounded. Get out of there!"

"We gotta go!" Liane pointed and Drew didn't question, just ran at her side as they both sprinted across the cavernous empty space inside the old storage shed and straight out the other side. There was someone lying on the ground, groaning and clutching at his leg; it was Cash.

Drew paused to lean over and take Cash's gun. "I'd stay down if I were you," he warned the biker. “This place is about to be overrun with ATF agents.”

“Fuck you,” Cash gasped, a thin sheen of sweat covering his face.

Liane blinked as Drew pulled his foot back and swung a kick into Cash’s injured leg. Then she understood as Drew said:

“That’s for the lump on my head, you asshole.”

Cash screamed, the sound high and thin, and then he apparently blacked out from the pain, slumping to the ground. Drew didn’t waste another glance on him, jerking his head to Liane. They ran, heading for the dock, hoping to give Hunter some backup and defend the hostages on the boat until the ATF strike team arrived.

“Your buddy’s already secured the boat,” Jessikah said, obviously seeing where they were headed. “He cast off a few seconds ago. Doesn’t look like he’s gotten the engine going but they’re drifting downriver and will be out of range in a minute or two. Don’t go that way, you’ll get stuck up against the water...”

Liane took a hard left, hissing Drew's name. They could hear shouting behind them, the occasional gunshot as someone took a wild shot, but she thought they'd lost the Brethren temporarily in the maze of the old mill's grounds.

"Get into the trees," Drew said quietly as they ran together, trying to keep their footfalls as quiet as possible. "We need to try and find Sasha and Emily, keep them safe. They don't even have shoes, they can't have got far."

"No shoes?"

"Frankly, I'm slightly surprised Gerry allowed them to keep any clothes."

Liane made a queasy face, thinking of the years of therapy those poor girls were going to need after this. She pressed a hand to her chest, feeling her breathing coming hard. Her chest still hurt like hell after taking the round to the vest, and she was sure she'd have one hell of a bruise when she took the vest off, but damn, she was glad Hunter had the spare in the trunk of his car.

"You okay?" Drew checked quietly, obviously having noticed her discomfort.

“Not the first time I’ve been hit in a vest,” she admitted. “It hurts, but I’ll be okay.”

They were at the treeline now and plunged in under the trees without breaking stride.

“Any hint of direction, Jess?” Liane checked.

“I got nothing, hon. Trees are way too thick. I’ve lost you too now. Best I can do is tell you if anyone else enters the woods from the mill site. Maybe. There’s a couple spots where the trees have encroached right up to the buildings...”

We’re on our own. Liane relayed the information to Drew quickly. They both slowed to a walk, moving as quietly as they could manage.

“Right.” He paused, looking back at the mill, tilting his head and obviously orienting himself. “They ran from there.” He pointed towards the building with the damaged roof, just visible from their location. “Went straight into the trees there. If they kept going straight... maybe we can intercept them if we go this way. Once your strike team get here and secure the mill, I’ll try calling out to them.”

Liane nodded, following him as he paced quietly deeper into the trees. She wasn't sorry at all to be moving away from the Brethren's stronghold and leaving the gang for the strike team to deal with, not considering how readily Bull had shot her.

"Drew!"

They both froze.

Kaleb, Drew mouthed, and Liane nodded. They couldn't see the young biker, but his voice was close. In the woods with them somewhere.

"Try and talk him down," she whispered.

Drew nodded and took a couple of cautious steps forward, gesturing for her to stay put. "That you, Kaleb?" he called, keeping his voice low.

"It's me, brother. What's going on?" Kaleb sounded plaintive. Lost. "You can't be working with the feds. I don't believe it. You're Jacob's cousin!"

"I am his cousin," Drew acknowledged, "and I know he was your friend, Kaleb, but Jacob and I didn't always see eye to eye."

“You betrayed us!”

Kaleb was pretty close, Liane thought, just off to their north. She made a soft sound, pointing in that direction when Drew glanced at her. He nodded. Made a gesture with his hand for her to circle around and try to get behind Kaleb, presumably while he kept the youngster talking. Quietly, she began to creep through the trees, doing her best not to let twigs crack under her feet.

“I’m sorry you feel like that, Kaleb,” Drew said, speaking a bit louder as he took another step forward.

“I thought you were my friend!”

“And I thought you were a basically decent kid who’d been led astray by bad company,” Drew said, his voice like iron.

Liane glanced back towards him, wondering where he was going with this.

“Until I saw the way you looked at that little Chinese girl.”

Oh. She winced, but kept going, slow and stealthy, creeping closer to the sound of Kaleb’s voice.

"Something's broken in you, Kaleb, because that's not right. We're not meant to feel that way about hurting other human beings, about hurting children."

Kaleb honestly sounded baffled when he replied "What the hell are you talking about? She's Chinese. It's not like she matters to anyone. There's nearly two fucking billion of the damn parasites..."

"Put your hands in the air," Liane ordered, stepping around a big tree and ramming the tip of her shotgun barrel against Kaleb's spine. "And don't give me an excuse to pull the trigger, you racist pedophile piece of scum."

The young biker froze, hands slowly raising. He had a gun, of course, and she reached up to relieve him of it - at which point, he moved quicker than she expected, twisting around and kicking out, aiming at her leg. It was a good hit and Liane's knee buckled under her. She scrambled backwards, instinctively trying to put some space between them, not ready to shoot Kaleb, her finger wasn't even on the trigger. She'd underestimated him and watched in horror as his gun hand came up.

Even if he hit her in the vest, at this range it was going to hurt a hell of a lot more than the earlier hit, and frankly, she suspected he was going to shoot her in the face.

Drew was close enough to see the struggle, not close enough to intervene - not bodily, anyway. There was only one choice he could possibly make, and he had no time to second-guess himself, to wonder if he could make the shot with only one good eye, because if he hesitated Kaleb was going to kill Liane. He closed his right eye, aimed and fired in a single smooth motion.

Liane watched the red hole bloom in the dead center of Kaleb's forehead. Saw his eyes go blank and dead before he dropped like a stone.

"Oh my God," she whispered.

"Liane?" Jessikah's panicked voice shouted in her ear. "Liane! That shot was way too close, what's going on?"

"Drew shot Kaleb," she said, her voice flat with shock. Her ears were still ringing and she could barely hear her sister.

"Your strike team arrived, and the Brethren are running for the trees. You might be about to have company. I can't help." Jessikah sounded stressed. "I can't see where you are, or where they are, but they'll have heard that shot. Be ready!"

"Incoming," Liane said succinctly to Drew, who was staring down at Kaleb's body, a look of regret on his face. "The strike team are at the mill and the Brethren are on the run."

"Kaleb!" a voice yelled close by. "Kaleb, where are you?"

"Bull," Drew said with a wince. "Not going to go well if he finds us standing over his nephew's body."

By unspoken, mutual agreement, they both turned and ran for it.

“We need to get back to the mill,” Liane hissed as they hurried through the trees. “The strike team are there. It’s the safest place right now.”

To her horror, Drew shook his head. “Not while Emily and Sasha are still out here. We gotta find them first, or they’re as good as dead.”

“Oh shit.” She really didn’t like it, but he was absolutely correct. Emily and Sasha would put every member of the Brethren in jail for life, if they lived to testify.

Behind them, a wordless roar of rage and grief went up; Bull had found Kaleb’s body. Then a hail of bullets suddenly started shattering through the trees. Bull had brought something heavier to the party, an AR-15 or similar from the sound.

“Get down!” Drew grabbed Liane’s arm, jerked her down to the ground as bullets streamed over their heads. Bull was firing blind, wild with fury, emptying the clip of his assault rifle without care where his shots went.

"You're hit!" She saw the blood on his sleeve. Drew looked at it uncomprehendingly, peeled the fabric back to show a bloody gash on his upper arm. It looked as though the bullet had grazed his bicep.

"It's fine. Keep moving."

The chatter of the gun fell silent. Magazine empty, Liane guessed, which meant Bull would need to pause and change it over. Assuming he was even carrying a second clip. Which surely he would be, she thought. Though considering his blind rage, maybe not. Maybe he hadn't been thinking about preserving ammunition.

"We need to go back. Try and arrest him," she whispered.

"Are you insane? No! He's pinpointed his location for the strike team," Jessikah snapped in her ear.

"No," Drew said at the same time. "He's not rational. If he sees either of us he'll try and kill us. Let your strike team take care of him."

A scream not far away took the decision out of their hands anyway; it was a woman's scream, and Liane highly doubted any other women were running around these woods other than Emily and Sasha. She lurched to her feet, grunting with pain as the bruise on her chest made itself felt again, and started running again, Drew beside her.

"Let her go!" another voice shouted, and they burst into a clearing to find Gerry dragging Emily out of a clump of bushes where she'd obviously been hiding and Sasha trying to fight him off with a tree branch.

"You heard Sasha. Let Emily go," Drew ordered, and Gerry turned on him with a snarl.

Chapter Twenty-Three

"You traitorous scumbag," Gerry spat at Drew, even as he quickly hauled Emily in front of him to use her as a shield, his gun digging into her ribs. The girl was crying, hopeless, desperate tears, and the sound tore at Drew's heart. He didn't have a shot, though, and couldn't risk it even if he did, not with that gun to Emily's side.

Liane had lowered her shotgun and now drew her pink Glock, holding it steady and tracking Gerry as he dragged Emily back towards the trees. Sasha dropped her tree branch, desperately calling her friend's name as she helplessly watched.

"Let her go," Drew said, keeping his voice calm, matter-of-fact. "You've done enough to that poor girl. Let her go, put your hands up, and you'll live to piss off the judge as you try to claim some sovereign citizen bullshit exempts you from justice."

"Fuck you," Gerry snarled.

"If you murder her in front of me, a federal agent, I will make it my personal mission to see that you suffer for the rest of your days in Florence Supermax until they take you to Terre Haute to end your miserable existence." Liane's voice was absolutely steady as she stared Gerry down. "Put the gun down and let her go."

"I'll kill her and I'll kill both of you too!" Gerry yelled.

"You're delusional. Pull that trigger and I'll blow your head off before you can pull it a second time. You gotta decide, Gerry, because you're only going to get one shot. Who's it going to be?"

Damn, she was smart, Drew thought, watching Liane taunt Gerry. Because Gerry would want either him or Liane dead much more than he wanted to kill Emily, and the second he took that gun away from Emily's side, Liane was going to take her shot. Drew could see her finger on the trigger, just waiting her moment.

"Yeah, Gerry." Drew added his taunts to Liane's. "You're beat and you know it. You can only take one of us."

Liane shot him a dagger glare for the briefest instant. He knew why - she was wearing a vest and he wasn't. If Gerry was going to shoot at anyone, she wanted it to be her. But she'd already been hit in that vest, its structural intensity was likely compromised... and Drew also knew that Gerry was a pretty good shot. He might well go for the head.

And the thought of Liane being shot in the head wasn't something Drew could live with, so he took a step towards Gerry.

"Kaleb's dead," he taunted. "I shot him in the head. Bull's crying his eyes out over the kid's body."

"You goddamn asshole." Real hurt showed on Gerry's face. "Kaleb believed in you."

"Kaleb was a raping pedophile who helped y'all kill and torture God knows how many innocent women and children." Drew's voice was cold. "I'd rather he lived to stand trial, but I don't regret taking the shot."

"Everybody freeze," an amplified voice boomed through the trees suddenly. "Federal agents! Put your weapons down and your hands in the air!"

Gerry looked around wildly, and Drew could see he was about to do something reckless. Emily seemed almost catatonic in his grip, limp. Gerry was exerting considerable strength to keep her upright and useful as his human shield.

"Come on, Gerry," Drew taunted, taking another step closer, careful not to get in Liane's line of sight. Every step he forced Gerry to take back opened the angle further, gave her a better shot without risking Emily. He just had to get Gerry to take that gun out of Emily's ribs. "Are you going down with a whimper, or out in a blaze of glory?"

Liane was going to murder him, if Gerry didn't. All Drew had to do was wait a few minutes and there'd be a dozen or more ATF strike team agents surrounding them. Gerry would see how hopeless his situation was and surrender. Surely.

"Emily," Sasha was sobbing, nearby. Liane moved to put herself between Gerry and Sasha, trying to shield the girl with her body. If Gerry shot Emily, they needed Sasha alive to tell her story.

"Stay back, Sasha," she said. "We got this. We'll get her."

Gerry was trying to back further into the trees, but loud voices announced the ATF agents were closing in, and he looked around wildly.

"It's over, Gerry," Drew said. "Just quit. Let Emily go."

"She's mine," Gerry snapped back. "She's coming with me." He grinned grotesquely. "We've had so much fun, haven't we, princess?" His hand gripped Emily's chin, tilted her face up, and he licked her cheek slowly. “So much fun. You wouldn’t want me to leave you behind.”

Emily’s eyes opened, and despite herself, Liane wanted to cringe away, because the despair and horror in them was beyond words.

“Let her go!” Drew yelled, and despite the fact that he didn’t have a good angle, he raised his gun, tried to get a bead on Gerry’s face. His arm was awash in blood, Liane saw then, realizing that his wound must be worse than they’d thought, but he didn’t so much as waver.

“Never,” Gerry snarled, and as he did, Emily seemed to come back to life. His grip on her face must have slackened just a little, and she twisted her head and sank her teeth into his hand with every bit of strength she had left in her weakened body.

“You little fucking bitch!” Enraged, Gerry howled with pain and tried to fling Emily away from him instinctively. She hung on doggedly, jaw clenched, even as she was thrown to the ground, and Gerry was forced to stoop over, to try and get his hand away from her ravaging teeth. His gun hand swung wildly, aiming for the briefest instant at nothing at all, and Liane took her shot. Took two, the double tap she'd trained endless hours for, the first shot drilling through Gerry's left eye and the second hitting an inch lower.

He was dead before he hit the ground atop Emily's fallen form.

"Shots fired!" someone bellowed close by.

"ATF agent Hagerty!" Liane yelled back, "neutralizing a threat!"

"Lower your weapon!" a voice screamed, and she turned to see a black-clad agent aiming his assault rifle at Drew.

"He's with me!" she shouted, quickly holstering her Glock, holding her hands up away from the shotgun. Drew was doing the smart thing, letting his gun dangle from his finger by the trigger guard, before bending slowly to put it on the ground.

Sasha had run to Emily, trying to drag her out from under Gerry's body as Emily shivered and sobbed with shock.

"Terrence?" Liane said, pretty sure it was the lead agent she knew, and the black-clad agent nodded, reaching up to pull down the black mask covering his mouth and nose. "Do you have Bull in custody?"

"The gang president? Yeah. Found him back there crying over another body." Terrence jerked his head. "Your handiwork too?"

"No, Drew shot Kaleb. Saved my life."

"Can I help them?" Drew gestured towards Emily and Sasha and Terrence nodded again, lowering his gun.

Liane went to help too, dragging Gerry's body off Emily with little care, despite knowing the crime scene investigators would be furious about it. Emily was more important now anyway, and Terrence was wearing a bodycam, so it wasn't as though what had happened was likely to be in dispute. She'd be buried in paperwork for a week or two, as always when an agent had to shoot someone in the line of duty, but everyone would agree Gerry had it coming.

"Get a medic," she told Terrence, "Drew's hurt. And Emily and Sasha need all the medical attention." And all the therapy, she thought but didn't say aloud, watching the two girls sobbing in each others' arms.

"I'm fine," Drew said, but he swayed slightly as he straightened back up, and she saw another gush of blood run down his arm.

"You are very not!" Grabbing his shoulder, she pushed him to sit down on the ground. "Sit down before you black out. We need to stop the bleeding."

Terrence provided a field dressing from his tac vest's pouches and a tactical earbud for Liane to listen in on, standing over them while reports came in of the rest of the gang being rounded up and Jason Hunter bringing the boat in to the dock, of more than thirty women and children on board sitting silently huddled together, awaiting their fate. Liane didn't know what would happen to them now, but she did know it would be a better future than whatever the Brethren had in mind for them. Especially for that one little girl Kaleb had selected. Liane hoped she never understood the grim fate that had awaited her at the Brethren's hands.

Liane sat on the ground with Drew's head in her lap, her hands holding the dressing against his arm to keep pressure on his wound. Watching Emily and Sasha clinging to each other and crying quietly, she realized had never felt so unutterably exhausted in her life. It was an enormous effort to keep her eyes open.

"Agent Hagerty," Terrence said, but his voice seemed to come from a very long way away. Liane blinked blearily up at him. "Are you alright?"

"I'm tired," she said. "Just. So tired."

"It's over," Drew said quietly, his uninjured arm moving, his hand coming up to cup her cheek. "It's all over, Liane. You can rest now. The job's over."

The job was far from over, she knew. The paperwork alone would consume weeks of her life, not to mention the debriefings, the classes she'd probably be asked to teach, and the court appearances she'd be called to make to testify if any of the surviving Brethren were stupid enough not to take whatever plea deals they were offered. Still, she closed her eyes and leaned into Drew's touch, savoring it for however long they had left.

Which turned out not to be long, as other ATF agents started arriving, one of them equipped with rather more medical gear than Terrence, and she heard the distant wail of a siren as an ambulance approached too.

"Liane." Someone crouched in front of her, and she blinked to bring Jason Hunter into focus. "You can let go now." He put a strong hand on hers. "Let the paramedics take him."

"Listen to him, Liane," Jessikah said in her earbud. She'd been quiet for the last little while, and Liane knew why; it was going to be tricky enough to explain to her bosses after the fact that Jessikah had basically been directing today's operation all along, while very probably being hacked into a satellite feed she had no business accessing. Liane wasn't looking forward to that conversation.

"You're going to be okay," Liane said reassuringly to Drew, who stared up at her with a not-at-all reassured expression on his face.

"I know I am, this is just a scratch. I'm worried about you. Go with Hunter, okay? Let him look after you."

"Okay," she said numbly, finally letting go of the dressing and letting Hunter lift her hand away. Within moments the paramedics were loading Drew onto a stretcher, taping a thicker dressing over his wound and rushing him away.

Emily and Sasha were being taken away too, coaxed along by two female ATF agents and a female paramedic, speaking to them in low, gentle voices and not trying to separate them for even a moment. That would come later, possibly much later. Liane wondered vaguely who would contact their families, tell them their missing daughters had been found. Explain the ordeal they'd undergone. Maybe Hunter; it was his jurisdiction, after all. Maybe the FBI.

"We still don't know who the mole is," she realized aloud.

"Leave it with me," Jessikah said in her ear. "I've got some ideas about where to look. Just waiting for someone to log Bull's phone into evidence and start scraping some data off it. Someone in the ATF, maybe. Who could give me access."

"I might know someone like that," Liane said, finding a smile. Hunter was looking at her oddly; she tapped her earpiece and he nodded, eyes flicking to Terrence and the other agents now surrounding them.

"Let's get you out of here," Hunter said, taking her arm to help her to her feet. "Get you somewhere safe where you can get a good night's sleep."

"Sleep," Liane said dreamily, "I haven't had a good night's sleep in... ever."

"Time you caught up, then."

"She's with us." Terrence caught at her other arm. "There's a plane on standby to take her back to DC."

"She's asleep on her feet!" Hunter snapped back. "The woman's worked her tail off living a double life for over a year for you lot. Even in the Rangers we gave men leave before we sent them back into action! At least let her have a damn night's sleep."

Terrence paused, seemed to really look at her for the first time. "It's probably not safe for her anywhere in Idaho awhile yet," he said regretfully. "Not until we've finished mopping up the rest of the Brethren's members and allies… all of whom she's identified for us. She can sleep on the plane, but I promise, I'll see she gets some rest before she goes back into the office."

"You do that." Hunter relinquished her arm at last. "Or you'll have to answer to Drew, and he's a lot scarier than me when he's angry."

Drew's not scary at all, Liane wanted to say, but she was honestly too tired to even force words out. She just let herself lean on Terrence's arm and staggered out of the woods, not caring any longer about needing to appear strong. She'd done enough. She'd done the job she'd come here to do, with Drew's help, and she was quite happy to leave the aftermath for the lawyers to clean up.

"Thank you for your help," she said to Hunter as she passed him, heard his laugh.

"Thank you, Agent Hagerty. For everything."

Chapter Twenty-Four

“Thank you, Agent Hagerty,” the Director said, nodding to her as she took her seat. “That was a very comprehensive report.” He looked around the table, at the other senior agency officials seated there. “Does anyone have any questions?”

“Why haven’t we heard from Drew Murphy?” one of the assistant directors asked.

“He’s not employed by us, and he declined our request to attend this debriefing.” The Director shrugged. “Considering the reports the Woodvale county sheriff’s department were kind enough to share with us, I believe we have all the information we might have received from his presence anyway. Well, if nobody else has any more questions,

I believe it's time we congratulate Agent Hagerty on a job well done. The agency received a lot of positive press coverage, the FBI and Border Force owe us some favors for breaking up a significant human trafficking operation, and there's a grateful state senator in Idaho who is very glad his niece is home. A very successful operation all around."

He hadn't mentioned the mole, Liane thought, but then, it was a little embarrassing to admit that a civilian had finally uncovered the Brethren's source... who had turned out not to be a DEA or FBI agent after all, but a congressman on a domestic intelligence committee. The man's wife was Bull's adoptive daughter from a previous relationship. Effectively functioning as her husband's private secretary, she had access to intelligence he never even bothered to read. It was Jessikah who had uncovered the link, of course; Bull's phone had turned out to be a dead end but Jessikah kept on digging, determined to find the mole, eventually joining the dots and finding her target. Liane had insisted on being present for the arrest.

"Lastly, of course," the Director continued, interrupting her reverie as he turned back to her, "there's the question of your next assignment."

"No," Liane said.

"I beg your pardon?" He raised his eyebrows, looking amused. "You're the golden girl right now, Agent. You can name your own choice of post. Whatever you want. Though," He eyed her hair, currently dyed pink with purple tips. "You might have to adapt your look a little if you want to progress up the ranks. You've got the ability to perhaps sit in my chair one day if you're prepared to put in the work."

"I'm sorry," she told him, "but I'm done."

"Done?"

Everyone around the table looked disbelieving.

"My notice." She slipped an envelope from her suit jacket pocket and laid it on the table.

"But... where will you go?"

"Still thinking about that. Maybe California. My sister's there." And Jessikah had been campaigning determinedly for Liane to join her firm, insisting that she'd both enjoy it more and get paid a lot more. She was still making her mind up, but whether she took the offer or not, she wanted to spend time with her sister. Get to know her again. And she was going to look up Drew, too, find out what he was doing now. It had stung that he hadn't accepted the request to come to DC for this meeting. She supposed he'd probably slotted right into a job as a regular deputy for Jason Hunter's sheriff's department, once the Brethren and their allies had all been scooped up, but she'd thought he might have reached out.

Maybe their relationship had been just a fling born out of desperation, of being the only two people who knew what their mission had been. The only other person each of them could trust.

Maybe Drew has already moved on. Found someone to settle down with.

I'm torturing myself. Stop it.

“Big sis!” Jessikah leaped up from her plush leather chair in front of a veritable wall of monitors - exactly how Liane had imagined her - and came forward with her arms spread wide to envelop Liane in an enthusiastic hug. “You made it!”

“Well, you did send me a first class ticket and even sent a driver to the airport to pick me up,” Liane remarked dryly, looking curiously around the office. “Though I admit, since it was an evening arrival, I thought he’d be taking me to your home rather than your work.”

The office block was about as anonymously nondescript as it was possible to get, in the middle of a large business park in Anaheim, surrounded by similar-appearing buildings. The only significant difference Liane had noted was that this building had no external signage. Or internal signage, come to that. Not a single thing to tell the casual onlooker - or slightly less casual snooper - what business occupied it.

Her escort from the airport, a grizzled older man who'd barely spoken a word for the whole drive, had swiped a keycard through half a dozen serious-looking security doors to let them in here. The sheer number of cameras discreetly mounted in every hallway and above every doorway let Liane know they took security very seriously… which was why it seemed odd that she hadn't been challenged in any way.

"Just what exactly is your role here? And in the interests of complete transparency, what exactly is here?" she asked her sister curiously, as Jessikah finally released her from the hug and waved her to a chair.

Jess smiled enigmatically. "Let's just say I'm more senior than you might expect from someone my age."

"And the business itself? You've been extremely vague about that." Liane leaned back in her chair and studied her sister. Jessikah looked good; she had always been a pretty girl, tall and slim as all three sisters had been, with sharply carved cheekbones, long dark hair drawn back into a long braid draping over one shoulder and dark blue eyes which always seemed to be glinting with amusement. As though Jess had secrets she wasn't about to share. A hoodie with an anime character on the front and raggedly cut off jean shorts hardly made her look like the senior executive she seemed to be implying she was, but Liane knew better than to judge someone by their clothes.

"We're a private security agency," Jessikah gave the same line she'd offered up when she'd told Liane she was quitting the NSA. "We take on a lot of jobs the government doesn't want to actively have its fingers in, as well as handling business for quite a few high net worth individuals."

"Business?" Liane made air quotes with her fingers. "Like personal security kind of business? Sounds a little dull."

"We do some of that, sure." Jessikah's smile was amused. "Sometimes they have pretty complex problems. We resolve them. Quietly and out of the media. It's pretty varied. Honestly, you can do whatever you like. Babysit an A-list celebrity or investigate a kidnap plot against a billionaire's brother. Authenticate multi-million dollar art or hunt down a gang dealing stolen anti-aircraft missiles."

Liane felt her eyes widen. Felt her body lean forward. She was giving away her interest, she knew. "Anti-aircraft missiles? Surely that's a job for the US military?"

"It might be. If they were American missiles." Jessikah's smile turned victorious. "They're not. But they might be being imported to use against US targets. It's a sensitive situation... and I thought your expertise might come in handy."

"You're offering me a job." She'd expected it, but she wanted to hear Jessikah spell it out.

"I am. Much better pay than you were getting. Bonuses. Holidays, top notch health care. The company will even find you an apartment, if you like." Jessikah waved a hand, as though to say, that stuff wasn't important. She knew her sister well. Liane didn't think any of that stuff was important. She wanted to know more about the anti-aircraft missiles.

"When can I start?" she asked, and Jessikah laughed.

“Right now, if you like. Welcome to Hestia Global Security, sis.” She leaned over, offering her hand.

“Hestia?” Liane queried. “The... goddess of the hearth?”

“Keeping the home fires burning,” Jessikah said cryptically, laughing again. “Oh. Would you like to meet your new partner?” Turning, she tapped a key on one of the keyboards on her desk, obviously setting off a signal somewhere else in the building, because a few moments later, the office door opened and a man stepped through.

Liane was halfway through protesting that she’d never worked with a partner and she didn’t need one now, when the words died on her lips. She stared disbelievingly.

“Drew?”

“Surprise.” He leaned against the doorframe, grinning at her. She’d put on a little weight, probably because she was no longer being run off her feet running the roadhouse as well as spying on the Brethren, and it looked great on her. Her pixie cut had grown out a little, curls dancing around her hairline, now dyed a fascinating shade of turquoise blue with black tips. "So, it turns out that your sister is really persuasive."

He'd spent a couple of nights in a hospital bed after the showdown with the Brethren when he got grazed by that bullet. It was the concussion he'd sustained from Cash smacking his head with the length of four-by-four that had concerned the doctors, especially since he didn't have someone to keep an eye on him at home... and his cabin had mysteriously burned to the ground while he was in hospital anyway, Hunter had stopped by to let him know. While Hunter had told him there'd be a job for him with the sheriff's department, they both knew there would be a target on his back if Drew stayed in Idaho. Too many people had vested interests in the Brethren's business and weren't best pleased they were no longer operating.

So when he'd walked out of the hospital after signing his own discharge papers and stopped at the kerbside to wonder where the hell he was going next, and a tall, beautiful young woman with decidedly familiar features opened her car door and beckoned him to get in, he was intrigued enough to walk over and let her say her piece.

He'd flown back to California with Jessikah that same day.

"You don't have to be partnered up, of course," Jessikah said when the silence stretched to an awkward length. "But I thought... since you've already worked well together..."

Liane shook off her apparent paralysis, leaped up from her chair, and practically flew across the room to throw herself on him. Grinning, Drew caught her, hugging her tight.

"I'll leave you to it," Jessikah said, slipping quietly from the room with a broad grin on her face as Liane's lips found Drew's.

“I can’t believe you’re here,” Liane murmured a little while later. Drew had led her from Jessikah’s office to another room, some sort of break room she thought, with a large and comfortable couch where they’d nestled down together to cuddle and talk.

“Turns out private companies don’t absolutely require their employees to have two working eyes.” Drew shrugged. “And like I said, your sister is very persuasive. She said she was trying to recruit you too, but wasn’t sure you’d leave the ATF.”

“I could feel myself being wedged into a little box. After so long basically being my own boss, I couldn’t do it any more. This,” she waved her hand to indicate the luxurious, but essentially anonymous office building, “I’m not a hundred per cent sure what this is, to be honest, but I am sure I’m not going to feel boxed in.” She traced her fingers gently along Drew’s jaw. “Getting to work with you will be amazing.”

“We did a pretty good job together, huh.” He grinned, leaning in to kiss her again.

"I really haven't ever worked with a partner much," she warned.

"Sure you have. We worked together for months in Idaho. You shot Gerry to save Emily and me."

"And you shot Kaleb to save me." She laced his fingers with his. "Do you regret it?"

"I regret the waste of his life. If he'd been raised in a different family, could he have been something other than what he was?" Drew shrugged. "Who can say? As he was, though... no, I don't regret it. The world's a better place without him, and sure as hell it's a better place without that scumbag Gerry."

"That's for damn sure!" Nestling her head against his shoulder, she said quietly "So we, what... get to pick our own missions now?"

"Something like that, but I think Jessikah has some specific things in mind she thinks we could help out with. I've been doing some recon and she's definitely onto something. We need to find and intercept those damn missiles before they end up in the wrong hands."

It was definitely the kind of mission to make any agent eager to get back into the field. Liane could feel her adrenalin rising just thinking about it. She grinned at Drew. "Think I could start next week?"

"Not tomorrow?" he teased.

"Well, I was planning on spending tomorrow in bed. With you, if you're free."

"I reckon I could clear my schedule."

Liane's laughter spilled over as she reached up to hook her arms around Drew's neck. "I missed you," she murmured against his lips. "More than I ever expected to miss anyone."

"I never thought I'd have anyone to miss me," he answered softly, "and I'm not truly sure how to go about this whole relationship thing, but I love you, Liane. What we have might not end up at picket fences and two point whatever kids, but wherever it goes... I'm all in."

All in. She liked the sound of that. Liked even more that Drew wasn't insisting on defining their relationship any particular way.

Partners. Lovers. Wherever they decided to take it… together.

"All in," she whispered back before pulling his mouth down to hers.

The End

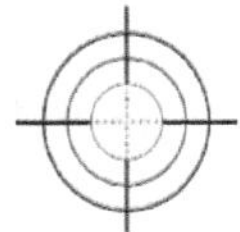

Thank you for reading Ranger's Mission! I hope you enjoyed Drew and Liane's story. The next book in the Rescue Rangers series will be Ranger's Blood, when Liane's outspoken, genius hacker sister Jessikah goes on her own undercover mission… with a former Ranger partner who's hellbent on keeping her safe, no matter what he has to do.

If you enjoyed Ranger's Mission, please do take a moment to leave a brief review on Amazon, Goodreads or Bookbub. Reviews are magic for authors and I very much appreciate anyone who takes the time to write one for my books!

You can find my web page at caitlynlynch.com. Pay a visit and sign up to my mailing list to be notified of my next scorching hot publication! I also share regular giveaways, tell you about super freebies and new releases from author friends of mine.

(You can unsubscribe at any time, and I promise not to spam you.)

Also By Caitlyn Lynch

RESCUE RANGERS SERIES

RANGER'S RESCUE

RANGER'S HOMECOMING

RANGER'S MISSION

RANGER'S BLOOD

SUNFISH ISLAND RESORT SERIES

FINDING CORY

THE RELUCTANT BILLIONAIRE

HER FAKE ISLAND WEDDING

SLOW SIMMER

FIGHTING FATE

RANGER'S MISSION

CROP IT LIKE IT'S HOT

STANDALONE BOOKS

IF WISHES WERE HORSES - AN IRISH ROMANCE

CAR CRASH LOVE

KITTENS FOR CHRISTMAS

DANA'S DUO

HOT FOR HEATHER

ELEVATOR ENCOUNTERS SERIES

ELLIE'S ENCOUNTER

JULIET'S ROMEO

THE BEST MAN FOR LEAH

RANGER HEAT SERIES

FIRST SUBMISSION

SECOND SURRENDER

THIRD THRILLS

www.ingramcontent.com/pod-product-compliance
Lightning Source LLC
Chambersburg PA
CBHW020946310726
48980CB00001B/73

* 9 7 8 0 6 4 5 1 8 2 8 8 0 *